CHASING
Sunsets

CHASING SUNSETS

J. E. JOYCE

A week in paradise, on the company dime, with your best friend - what could be better? How about a night with the ex-military SCUBA instructor? Or what if it turns into more than just a night?

Gabriel wanted nothing more than to escape the same old, lonely day-to-day he always faces. When he and his best friend, Deepa, decide to spend an extra week in paradise and get in a couple of adventures after their work conference, he never would have guessed he would find himself tongue-tied and stupid, on his knees, at the feet of their drop-dead gorgeous and cranky as hell SCUBA instructor. Jesus, Mary, Joseph, Sonny, and Cher... this wasn't how this trip was supposed to go.

Cade wasn't even supposed to be the one leading this little diving excursion, but when his roommate turns up MIA and calls in a favor, he finds himself tripping over a silver-haired little shark in the waters of his perfectly controlled life. Quiet, stoic, and all too serious. His life doesn't have room for noise, color, or distractions. Until Gabriel turns up literally at his feet, forcing Cade's cranky self into a full-on Technicolor world, at least for the weekend. But what if he wants to be more than just a vacation fling for this little shark?

Portions of this story were released under a different pen name as part of an anthology that has been out of print for a few years. While some scenes may feel familiar, names, settings, and characters have been changed. The story as a whole has been heavily edited and expanded by almost three times the length. I loved the initial bones of this story and always wanted to give these men the happily ever after they deserved. I can't think of a better couple to be the first one I get to introduce you to as J.E. Joyce. I truly hope you fall in love with them as much as I have.

*To all of us who have lost our
way in the last few years,
May you find your joy and
stop merely chasing sunsets*

"IF I HAVE to listen to one more person say the word 'agile' in any other context than a dirty one, I am going to lose my fucking mind," my best friend Deepa says with an overdramatic groan. She may be the one person on the planet who I am allowed to call overdramatic. No one beats my dramatics when I go into full Kween mode... which happens frequently. Maybe too frequently. And entirely unapologetically.

"Buttercup, is 'agile' the adjective you really want to be striving for? I can think of much better qualities in a bedmate," I ask, showing genuine concern for her love life. Or should I say lack thereof, knowing full well this bitch is in just as bad of a dry spell as my no-longer-as-perky ass.

"Not all of us have the luxury of being ridiculous size queens, my love. Some of us mere mortals have gone long enough without a good dickin' we'll settle for 'has a pulse and takes direction mildly well,'" Dee retorts, throwing a snark-filled eye roll over her shoulder as she sweeps out of the large glass double doors leading from the conference center out into the blinding Hawaiian sun.

We've spent the last five days, ten hours a freaking day, locked in class, after breakout session, after keynote speech, at a tech conference the software development firm we both work for sent us to. Ah yes, nothing quite so glamorous as sitting in drab conference rooms, breathing recirculated tech geek sweat stink, with the mandate to bring your "valuable new insight and expertise" back to the home company because some executive got a bug up their ass that this particular conference is going to unlock the holy grail of here-to-fore undiscovered wells of developmental productivity. *insert massive eye roll here* yeah. Because this yearly conference absolutely isn't an exact rehashing of the same shit we've been doing for the last ten years. It could be worse, at least. Last year they held the conference in Hoboken. A week all on the company's dime in Hawaii with my bestie, um, yes, please!

We aren't even ten feet from the conference center doors before Deepa steps off to the side of the walkway and starts digging through the giant Mary Poppins-looking bag she's been toting around all day.

"Has a pulse and takes direction mildly well?" I tease, stepping over and hip-checking her, maybe putting slightly more force behind it than is absolutely necessary on the off chance it would knock her off balance and make her tip over into the sand in a crazy bag lady heap. Come on; I've been listening to old men with beer bellies they think their belted polos and front pleated khakis somehow magically disguise, drone on and on about project management strategies, agile methodology, and scrum engagement. And not a single one had the decency to pull up a picture of a bunch of sweaty rugby players in those tiny little shorts to show a proper scrum. Rude. I deserve a little entertainment as a reward for pretending to pay attention all day. If that involves playing my own little version of cow tipping, then so be it.

"Hateful bitch!" she snaps, glaring at me as she holds out her hand impatiently. "And yes, if I have to deal with one more man rubbing the shit outta my pubic bone two inches to the left of even being in the same zip code as my clit, I will lose my damn mind."

"And you call me a hateful bitch?" I laugh, tugging the white oxford shirt with the subtle purple check pattern from my waistband and over my head before slapping it into Dee's waiting hand. "Frankly, I don't blame the men. Women's genitals are entirely too complicated. It's a wonder any of you get off... or aren't all lesbians."

Since today was the last day of the conference, we agreed we wouldn't waste a single second once the last session let out before hitting the beach and getting the biggest, fruitiest drinks we could get our hands on. In that spirit, we came prepared. Under my business casual appropriate oxford, I have on my *Sounds Gay... I'm In* light blue tank that still works perfectly with my slim cut gray jeans and ankle boots; thank you very much. Dee tosses my latest geeky indulgence with one hand toward me as she shoves my shirt into her bag with the other. Before coming on this trip, I splurged and bought myself a pair of the sunglasses Crowley wears in the Good Omens TV adaptation on Amazon. David Tennant gives me LIFE as Crowley.

"Well, we can't all be day-drinking power bottoms

like you, now, can we?" Dee sasses back as she unzips the prim little gray number she wore for the conference, revealing the skin-tight white tank and black lycra running shorts underneath.

With a less than dignified squeaking gasp, I snatch the flouncy little teal Hawaiian print skirt she was about to tug on before huffing, "Don't you DARE disrespect our lord and savior Loki like that!"

"... You watched Thor Ragnarök again last night, didn't you?" she asks with an eye roll as she snatches her skirt back and tugs it on quickly.

"It's easily the best movie to come in the MCU canon, and you know it," I defend haughtily.

"Whatever you say, babe. We seriously need to get you laid. You are reaching unhealthy levels of nerd. Before you know it, I am going to find you playing World of WarCraft in your mother's basement, screeching about the 'goddamn noobs ganking my shit!'"

"There are so many things wrong with what you just said; I don't even know where to start. But let's be honest, it would have to be in *your* momma's basement because at least she acknowledges my existence," I say with a wink.

Dee pauses, pulling her mass of waist-length jet-black hair into a high ponytail, staring at me with a horrified look. "Shit, I'm sorry, love. I wasn't thinking... you know I don't mean..."

"Oh shush, I know, I know. I know you don't mean anything by it. And you know, as far as I'm concerned, I magically appeared as a fully formed Lady Glitter Sparkles Homo Supreme. No parents included or necessary."

"But still..." Dee tries again, genuine remorse shining in her big dark eyes.

"Seriously, shush. We both know I'm Mama Suman's favorite child anyway," I tease, tugging the giant bag from her grip and slinging it over my shoulder, ready to get a move on to get my drink on.

"That may be true, but I've always been Baba's girl anyway," Deepa laughs as she rushes to catch up to me.

"Naw, Baba Vinod loves me too," I say, pushing my sunglasses into place as the sidewalk opens to the main walkway between the conference center and the resort.

"Yeah, yeah. We all know you are the beloved daughter they never had." I can hear the eye roll in her voice as she pulls up next to me, slipping her hand into the crook of my arm. "So now, oh favorite Singh daughter, what's on the docket tonight?"

"I need something big and fruity shoved in my face after that boring-ass closing keynote," I groan, directing us toward one of the poolside bars overlooking the beach.

Dee gives an unladylike snort beside me and almost trips over her own feet as she laughs. "Something big and fruity, huh? Oh god, Gabriel, that one's almost too easy!"

"Shut up, bitch. You know what I meant. We need drinks, then dancing," I say in my most haughty tone, attempting to look down my nose at her.

"Let's grab a drink here, then uber it into town and find a club. Momma needs to get her groove on!" Dee crows, doing an awkward little shimmy thing as we step up to the open-air bar.

"Stella, 1998 called, and they want their phrase back."

"God, you really are a hateful bitch when you need a drink. Are we even old enough to be using that movie as a reference?" she snarks before stepping onto the footrail along the bottom of the bar so she can lean across the cement bar top inlaid with shells in swirling patterns.

"Shush your mouth! How Stella Got Her Groove Back is a classic! Queen Angela Bassett, Whoopi, and don't even get me started on the deliciousness that is young Taye Diggs."

"K, white boy," she says with an eye roll, dismissing me.

Giving up on the argument, we slip into easy conversation about the conference as we wait for our drinks. We are halfway through the giant blue concoctions before we finally change subjects again.

"Alright. We are here for another week. No more work talk," Dee declares, slapping her hand onto the bar as if that seals her proclamation.

"Deal. Escaping that frozen hellscape to gallivant around on the beach may be the best idea we have ever had. I was about to lose my mind if I had to spend another morning digging my car out of waist-high snowdrifts before work." I raise my glass in cheers, already knowing the decision to burn some of my saved-up vacation days and run away to the sand and sun was exactly what I needed.

"Yes, because the snow is the only thing you hate about being back home," she teases.

"Don't even go there. You and I both know how much I need to recharge and reset after the holidays. It sucks spending 'family holidays' alone. Eggnog for one... no fun."

"First off, eggnog? Gross. Never say that to me again. Second, I would kill for a holiday with some peace and quiet. Mata Suman may try to mention the odd 'such a nice boy' to you here and there, but can you even imagine what it's like dealing with Ma going on and on about how I'm not getting any younger and all she wants is to see her grandbabies before she gets too old and frail to enjoy them. Not to mention Baba saying he needs to find me a 'good strong man' to take care of me. Oh, and let's not forget Madhav, the perfect little Indian son that he is, with his supermodel-looking wife and litter of ankle-biters." Her rant is barely over before Dee lifts the giant hurricane glass and downs the second half of her drink in one go. Her family and their expectations as their only daughter have always weighed on her. Since we both turned thirty a couple of years ago, her parents have upped their guilt game and turned into crazed matchmaking fiends. Some serious horror stories have come out of that mess, but that's for another time.

"Point taken. We both agree that holidays suck, and being on the beach to decompress after that insanity was brilliant. Moving on," I declare, taking another swig of my unabashedly fru-fru concoction of wonderfulness. "I have an idea, well, more of an edict if you will, but I enjoy making you think you have a say in matters now and again."

"So magnanimous of you. I salute your efforts," Dee deadpans, giving me a one-fingered salute. Lifting her glass for another drink, she gets it all the way to her face before realizing it's empty. With a comically over-exaggerated pout, she slams the glass back on the table, adjusts so she's flipping off the glass instead of me, and gripes. "Why is the rum always gone?"

Waving down a passing server, I do the universal magical wave across the table, signaling for refills before turning to her and placating, "Calm yourself, Captain Jack. Daddy has you covered."

Dee gives a less-than-dignified snort and almost falls off her stool as she laughs, "You *wish* you were a Daddy."

Scrunching up my face, I have to agree. "No, you're right. More like I want to find one... but no self-respecting Daddy wants an over-the-hill former twink for a boy."

"Over-the-hill former twink?! Jesus, Gabriel, you make it sound like you've got one foot in the grave!" she scolds.

"I might as well have! I'm ancient in gay years! Ancient, I tell you!" My overdramatic old Hollywood starlet impression is on point tonight; if I do say so myself, thank you.

With an eye roll, Dee wads up the now soggy cocktail napkin from under her drink and lobs it at me. "Dear god, you're exhausting. You're thirty-three. Not dead. Calm your tits."

"I most certainly will not!" I scoff, not ready to let go of my tizzy. Knowing me entirely too well, Dee only lifts a skeptical brow as she stares me down, looking thoroughly unimpressed with my antics.

I'm about to argue again when fresh drinks are placed before us. Taking a sip, I give in with a sigh. "Fine, if I must. But I'll only calm one. Not this one, though," I say, lifting my palm to cup my nonexistent left breast. "This one's my party tit."

To her credit, Dee only rolls her eyes and takes another long drink. Unfortunately, I think I scared our poor server to death because the girl made a terrified choking sound before staggering into the crowd with a horrified look.

"Are you done terrorizing the locals?"

"Not even remotely, let's be honest. But that brings me back to the subject at hand," I explain with an excited smirk.

"What? Your party tit, or lack thereof?"

"Hateful bitch," I mutter, taking another drink before once again attempting to explain my plan. "So, as I have been trying to say... we have eight days left on the island. My idea is we each need to do something unexpected. Something we would never do at home."

I see Dee about to argue, so I press on, cutting her off before she has the chance. "Before you go poking holes in my idea, hear me out. In the spirit of all fairness, we would have to do each activity together, plus I refuse to let you ditch me for some skanky hookup all week."

"My hookups are not skanky!" she cries. Using her own look against her, I stare back with my best impression of her skeptical brow raise I can muster until she gives in. "Okay, not *all* my hookups are skanky. Bitch," she grumbles.

"No judgment from me, you know I've had my fair share of skanks in my past... fuck, I've *been* the skank on more occasions than I care to count at the moment... but that's all beside the point. The point is, I am suggesting we each get to choose an activity we have to do together this week. Something we would never do at home or never think to do on our own. We need to get out of our comfort zones and live a little before heading back to our boring-ass lives."

Dee seems to mull over my proposal for a few moments, running her finger idly along the rim of her glass. Eventually, she asks, "So, you'd have to do whatever I pick?"

I recognize that evil twinkle in her eyes, and I am NOT having it. "Slow down there, Satan. We *both* have to do whatever we pick. No sending me to freebase into a volcano or something. Unless you have some weird Joe Versus the Volcano fantasy you're dying to live out, or something that is.... Please say no. I can't pull off that flowered sarong getup Meg Ryan rocks in that one."

"Wait... why would you get to be Meg?"

My glass pauses mid-air on the way to my mouth, and I gape at Dee. "That's a rhetorical question, right? Between the two of us, which one is more likely to have a mental breakdown and start screaming at the moon while the other sleeps peacefully at their feet? Yeah. Exactly. Shut up, Tom."

Dee mumbles a curse under her breath before squaring her shoulders and facing me again.

"Two things. One, call me Tom Hanks again, and I'll kill you. Two, I'm in. Having a couple of adventures while we are here sounds surprisingly great. I'd love to sit on the beach all day, don't get me wrong, but getting out and doing something sounds too good to pass up."

I have to admit, as much as I love my bestie, I figured there was about a fifty-fifty chance of her shutting me down. I mean, I am absolutely the princess between the two of us, but Dee has never met a lounger and e-reader she didn't love. Neither of us is necessarily what you would call the 'adventurous type,' but honestly, that's part of why I suggested this little plan. I don't want to waste our time away, I want to get out of my comfort zone at least a little, and I know I can't be trusted to drag myself there... hence forcing Dee to be my battering ram.

"To not being lazy asses all week!" Dee cheers, raising her glass for a toast.

Clinking my glass against hers, I cheer, "To dragging your ass off the beach!"

CHAPTER TWO
GABRIEL

I'M GOING to kill her. I will strangle her, chop her up into little pieces, and serve her over rice with a nice curry. I bet Mama Suman would make her killer samosas if I ask nicely; those would go perfectly with a nice Curry a 'la Deepa.

We officially made it to day four of our vacation before the bitch drove me to homicide. Actually, I'm surprised I made it this long.

We agreed to spend the weekend doing absolutely nothing other than sitting on the beach and drinking fruity drinks served to us by muscle-bound pool boys. I know this little adventure plan was my idea. Still, I have to admit, the thought of staying here and watching those tight asses in even tighter shorts bringing me drinks all week sounds rather amazing right now. Especially after the little stunt Dee just pulled.

Yesterday we agreed to celebrate being on the island while the rest of our schmuck co-workers were back in the office by completing my chosen adventure.

Growing up in the Pacific Northwest, you end up with an appreciation for the outdoors and hiking, whether you like it or not. It's in the place's lifeblood. So naturally, I decided we should go hiking. After talking to the delightfully rambunctious little cutie behind the concierge desk, I found a popular trail hike that ends at a waterfall. The views were stunning, and getting out into the jungle was seriously incredible. I thought Dee would appreciate swimming in the waterfall pool.

I. Was. Mistaken.

I have never in my life seen someone despise being in nature as much as that ridiculous wench. I swear to Our Lady of Peace, our Lord and Savior Gaga, Dee started bitching the second we stepped out of the rental car and only progressed to full-on threats of bodily harm and death by the time we got to the falls. Do you know how hard it is to get your swim on while a tiny angry woman yells curses at you in Hindi?

Should I have expected retribution? Absolutely. Did I expect my best friend to turn into a heartless harpy witch and completely abandon me to my death in the dark abyss? Absolutely fucking NOT.

Fish and other creepy-crawly sea creatures have never been my favorite. Don't get me wrong, I love going to the aquarium as much as the next gay. But I am a firm believer that they have their world, and I have mine, and as long as we both stay where the sweet baby Jeebus intended, we can all get along just fine.

So naturally, what does Dee choose for her little outing? Why, SCUBA diving, of course.

The diving itself might not have been so bad if the little traitor hadn't ditched me at the last second, leaving me stranded and standing on this dock like a moron, waiting for our guide to show up.

I hate her.

When we got home from the hike yesterday, she demanded I leave her alone the rest of the night while she took, and I quote: "the longest soak known to man, with every bath bomb I can get my hands on, and attempt to deal with all these damn bug bites. All of which are *your* fault."

Drama, thy name is Deepa.

I honestly wasn't expecting to see her till at least lunch today, figuring she would want to sleep in and make me sweat as long as possible. So, when I got a knock on my hotel door this morning at nine, the last thing I was expecting to find was Dee holding two cups of coffee on the other side.

"Get up, asshole. We need to be at the pool in twenty minutes. Get going."

"Well, good morning to you too, sunshine," I grumble, turning back to the room, leaving her to follow and close the door behind her.

"Yeah, yeah, good morning. Hurry up. I don't want us to be late," she snaps, setting the drinks on the dresser before flopping ever so ungracefully onto the unmade bed.

Glancing over my shoulder at her as I dig through the drawer for a dry pair of swim shorts, I can't resist fucking with her a little. She woke me up, after all. "You're brave. For all you know, I could have spent the night making sweet, sweet love in those sheets, and now there you go, rolling around in my sex mess."

A pillow connects with the back of my head, and I hear the sheets rustling as she makes herself more comfortable. "Sugar, you and I both know the only sweet loving you got last night was with yourself."

Well. Fine, then. I mean, she's not wrong, obviously. It's been goddamn months since I got laid. But she doesn't have to be so... blatantly rude about it. Because she is clearly still pissed at me for yesterday, I decide not to care about her delicate sensibilities, shuck off the cotton sleep shorts I'm wearing, and step into the little powder blue swim shorts I bought, especially for this trip. Think Daniel Craig stepping out of the Mediterranean in Casino Royale, or as I like to call it, the moment you heard millions of nonexistent gay boy ovaries explode all around the world.

"Goddammit, Gabriel! We both know your ass is better than mine; no need to rub it in. And if I catch you hanging brain around me one more time, I swear to Shiva I will rip that shit off," Dee barks from the cocoon of pillows and blankets she has made for herself in the center of my bed.

"Well, you're the one building a nest in my room while demanding I get ready. I can't help it if you see the goods. Not my fault you're a dirty little voyeur," I scoff, throwing on a lightweight zip-up hoodie and stepping into my flip-flops.

"Oh, you know what I like," Dee purrs sarcastically as she rolls off the bed, attempting to untangle herself from the comforter wrapped around one leg and her coverup twisted around her waist.

"Jesus, you're a mess. Come on, munchkin, let's head out before the blankets devour you." I grab my coffee from the dresser and head to the hallway without looking back, leaving Dee to catch up. I'm halfway down the hall when the sound of her flip-flops smacking furiously and the slam of a door lets me know she vanquished the horrible duvet beast and is catching up.

Turns out, my now former best friend signed us up for a private SCUBA diving excursion. Traitorous bitch. We had a two-hour crash course private lesson at the resort pool in the morning, hence the early wake-up call. After the lesson, we were told to meet at the marina at two this afternoon for the actual dive.

I must admit, the pool session this morning was rather fun. Being able to putter around the pool for an hour without needing to come up for air was surprisingly entertaining. The difference is, in the pool, it's not only crystal clear, but it's also blissfully chlorinated to guarantee no creepy crawlies live in there. The ocean, though? That's their home. The fish, and the sharks, and the giant octopi squid things that will suck your face off at the slightest provocation. They all live there, and we are invaders. How well have invaders been treated by the locals throughout history? Yeah. Think about that, dammit.

And now the bitch has abandoned me to have my face sucked off by horrible sea creatures alone. When I stopped by her room before heading to the marina, I found her wrapped up in bed, claiming to be miserably sick. Yeah, I would be much more willing to believe her if she hadn't been shamelessly flirting with, and all but throwing herself at, the gorgeous local leading our diving lesson this morning.

I'm not sure why I even came without her. If she can fake sick, I should be able to as well. But Dee is evil and knows when she uses her "power pout" I can't say no. So here I am, standing around like an idiot, consoling myself with the fact I will at least get to spend the day with the gorgeous, albeit straight, instructor from this morning.

The sound of footsteps coming up behind me pulls me from my morbid thoughts, and I turn to face my fate.

"Holy Manu Bennett!" I gasp, clutching my chest like the diva I am.

Did I fall in the water and get eaten by the Kraken already and not realize it?! Because striding down the dock toward me is Crixus from Spartacus in black board shorts and aviator shades.

Is this heaven? This must be heaven.

As if my diva gasp wasn't a stellar enough first impression, in my haste to clutch at my nonexistent pearls, I drop everything I had been holding. The contents of my beach tote go rolling across the dock between us, sending my $54 bottle of Sephora sunscreen off the side and into the murky depths below.

The choice between dignity and overpriced skincare products is no choice at all. I drop to my knees and scramble to shove everything back in my tote before anything else gets sacrificed to Ursula. As I shove my backup hydro flask into the bag, a pair of tanned flip-flop-clad feet stop in front of me.

I swear my brain disconnects from my body, and I lose all control over my limbs. Before I know what's happening, I'm staring into the reflective lenses of an Adonis in a black rash guard that's all but painted onto his defined chest and torso.

"Holy Crixus on a cracker," I breathe on a dreamy sigh, like a complete idiot.

The warm roll of his laughter startles me out of my stupor, and I scramble to shove the last of my things into my bag and jump to my feet. It's only when I wobble unsteadily on my feet I realize how close we are, my shoulder brushing against a solid pectoral. Snapping my head up with what I'm sure is a horrified look on my face, I try to step back, but he steadies me with a hand on my shoulder and an arched brow peaking over the rim of his sunglasses.

"Crixus, huh? Can't say I've heard that one before, but I'll take it. I can get behind some Spartacus." As if his laugh wasn't enough, his voice melts every cell in my body and kills off what little brain power I had left. It's deep and rich, like warm melted chocolate and whisky running down the back of my throat.

Speaking of running down the back of my throat, I would love to have something else of his...

"You alright?" he asks, that brow behind his shades only rising higher. I swear it's reached The Rock levels of brow raise.

"I... uh..." Seriously, all higher brain functions have completely abandoned me. What. The. Fuck.

"Cool, good talk," Manu says, sarcasm dripping in every syllable as he steps around me and climbs onto the boat behind us.

Well. That did it. Like a perfectly calibrated "asshole switch," my brain pops back into a functional mode, and the Manu look-a-like goes from swoon-worthy to punch-worthy in two seconds flat. I square my shoulders, call upon the sass of all the drag queen divas that came before me, and stomp my way onto the boat after the asshole.

Would my little diva stomp entrance have been more effective if the entire boat hadn't rocked when I stepped onto the deck and sent me careening into a wall? Absolutely. Did I recover like the queen I am and strut my fine ass up to a bench along the side of the boat like it's my job? You bet I did. Slamming my bag down on the bench next to me, I sit down and cross my legs primly before finally turning to address the ass, now fiddling with the controls at the command center thing in the center of the open boat.

"What happened to Teo? I thought he would bring us out today," I ask, doing my best to sound haughty and unaffected. Teo was the instructor this morning for the crash course at the pool. The gorgeous man Dee spent the entire lesson shamelessly throwing herself at.

"He came down with something. I'm Cade, his business partner. I'll be taking over," he answers bruskly, not even bothering to look up from the controls. The engine roars to life, cutting off any response I may have had and sending a clear message. Cade is not one for a chat.

Great. Today should be fun.

An hour later, we are anchored on the edge of a secluded reef. Cade briefly explained this area is named Three Fingers, and I, being the twelve-year-old pre-pubescent boy that I am, giggled. That little show of dignity earned me an *'are you serious?'* look and an abrupt end to the meager amount of conversation we had going. Cade quickly got the gear set up and helped me wrestle my way into the BC and air tank that had me all but tipping over backward. I now stand at the edge of the boat's back deck, staring down at Cade's grumpy-as-shit face bobbing in the gentle waves below as he yells at me to jump in.

Jump in. Just jump in. Sure, yeah. He makes it sound so easy, as if it's not plummeting into the depths of the unknown with a giant metal weight strapped to my back. Yeah, I'll get right on that, thanks.

"Come on, we don't have all day. Put your regulator in. One hand holds the front of your BC, the other presses against the regulator and your mask to hold them in place. Then just take one big step off the boat."

Regardless of the fact he has been a grumpy son of a bitch since we got on the boat, I can't deny his voice cuts through the nervous buzzing in my head. Replaying his instructions in my mind, I take a slow, deep breath and execute each step with careful movements.

"Good, good. Hold your gear, and now... STEP!" he calls, his voice forceful and commanding. Before I realize I'm moving, my body follows his command. I fall for a moment before hitting the water in a rush. Thanks to the gear and my frantic instinct to kick my finned feet, I quickly pop up to the surface. I can't help but laugh around the regulator still clenched between my teeth, inflating my BC like Teo instructed.

"See? Not that hard. Okay. We are going to head down now. Follow me and stay close," he directs. We hurry through some basic hand signals Teo taught Dee and me this morning. Once Cade is satisfied, I know the basics, he takes up his regulator and motions for me to follow him down.

I take one last open breath before I fit the regulator in my mouth, clear any remaining seawater from it, and release the air from my BC, sinking slowly beneath the rolling waves. Cade is hovering about ten feet below, waiting for me to catch up before going any further.

When I reach him, he motions forward and waves for me to follow before turning and swimming at a downward angle, away from both the boat and shore beyond. Knowing I have already come this far, and Dee will never let me hear the end of it if I waste all the money she dropped on this private dive, I take a slow deep breath, and follow Cade down.

The boat is anchored above a patch of relatively clear sand about twenty feet below the surface. As we swim out toward the reef, the patchy groupings of rock and coral become more frequent and more extensive. There are a few fish darting between coral outcroppings, but nothing all too exciting, really. I catch myself feeling the beginnings of annoyance, wondering what the big deal is about diving.

No sooner than those thoughts enter my mind, we cross a ridge, and the sight before me steals my breath completely. Cade and I hover just above the edge of a small drop off, the sheer face of the coral wall sinking roughly another twenty feet below us. Beyond that, there is a riot of color, life, movement, and overwhelming beauty. Large boulders and coral formations are growing all into and around one another to form the massive reef that seems to stretch out as far as the near-perfect visibility the calm waters are affording us. If I could gasp and trust my regulator wouldn't fall out of my face, I would.

Once again, Cade motions to follow, and he takes off down the ridge, sinking into the reef below. For a moment, I wonder if I should freak out right now. I am literally surrounded by all manner of sea creatures, and god knows what is hiding in the massive coral with all its nooks and crannies. Taking stock of my emotions and mental state, though, I find I don't have it in me to be afraid. It's all too beautiful to be scared. I want nothing more than to soak it all in, to see everything there is to see... and I find myself with an overwhelming need to see a turtle. I'm not sure why, but seeing a turtle while I'm down here feels imperative.

CHAPTER THREE
GABRIEL

DEE and I are lounging in a Bali Bed down by the pool the next morning, enjoying the breeze coming off the water. We had an argument when we first came down; the tension still high from yesterday's shenanigans. I wanted to spend the day on the beach. In my mind, she owes me whatever the hell I want today for ditching me so unceremoniously yesterday. Dee thinks she did me some grand favor and feels not one hint of remorse for being a terrible, horrible, no good friend. She didn't want to be on the beach with the breeze the way it is, so naturally... we are up here by the pool because I'm a giant pushover underneath all this bravado. And If I am completely honest with myself, I can't really find it in myself to be angry with her.

Something inside me shifted yesterday. Not only did I face what I once thought was my deepest fear, but I felt my world shift on its axis for the first time since I held Connor Dornan's hand in first grade, he kissed my cheek, and I realized I liked boys. As I swam through the maze of coral formations yesterday, I realized I wanted more, more than the stagnant, quiet life I've been stuck in for entirely too long. Sure, I have a decent job that I don't completely hate, a decent apartment, and an admittedly fantastic group of friends. While that may be all well and good for now, it's not going anywhere. There is nowhere to go, no progress to make, and no *life* in any of it. I have no family. I can't remember the last time I went on a date, and it's been even longer since I had a good tumble.

At the risk of sounding like that damn redheaded mermaid... I want more.

Something cold and wet smacking me in the forehead drags my attention back to the present, and Dee lounging next to me with a confused scowl.

"What the hell was that for?!" I screech, rubbing the wet spot on my forehead and brushing an ice cube from where it landed on my stomach.

"You were humming '*Part of Your World*' with one of those creepy thousand-yard stares you get when you zone out."

"I was not!" I counter, though I know it's pointless. This wouldn't have been the first time I've randomly broken out in Disney songs while lost in thought. Hey, if they didn't want me to sing them, they shouldn't have hired so many Broadway divas to voice them. Give me Queen Lea Salonga any day.

"Yeah, sure, honey. So, you gonna tell me what has you so utterly shook today? Or are you gonna keep pretending to be pissed at me and expect me to believe that's it?" This woman knows me entirely too well and can read me like an open book. Dammit. I should have known I wouldn't get away with playing my internal crisis off as nothing but a shit fit.

With a deep breath, I give in, knowing it will be less painful to just get it over with than put up with her nagging all day. "So... You know how... Are you...? I mean..."

Dee cuts me off with several repeated slaps to the chest as she sits bolt upright on our lounger bed and shoves her giant sunglasses up into her hairline. "Love you, totally care about your crisis, but look. Look over there. Told you sitting up here was a perfect choice today!" Dee all but squeals as she takes another sip of her overly boozy fruity drink through an honest to god curly straw.

"What the hell are you..." I sputter, waving off her attack.

"Argue later. Look now!" she hisses, pointing oh so subtly to the other side of the pool. A group of workers is building another set of Bali Beds on what is apparently a newly renovated section of the resort grounds. There are five men, all shirtless, all glistening with sweat in the mid-morning sun, and all completely gorgeous. Dee has a point. My problems pale compared to the prime showing of eye candy unfolding before us.

"Think if I turn up the music on my phone, it will get them to do a little dance for us?" she asks, nodding her head sharply once to settle her sunglasses back into place so she can stare in peace.

"They already have a radio going. Can't you hear it?" I counter, unwilling to admit I would be entirely on board with watching those men shake what their mommas gave them.

Dee and I settle comfortably against the back cushion of the bed, each of us hiding behind our sunglasses and giant drinks to watch the show, adding in our own color commentary as we go. The men are obviously locals, and four of the five must have at least some level of Pacific Islander blood in them for their dark coloring. As for the fifth, I would believe him wholeheartedly if he introduced himself as Ragnar, the Viking Lord.

I'm not entirely sure how long we sit and watch them work like the horrible creepers we are, but I know our drinks were refilled by the cute cabana boy at least once. That, and the lack of breakfast, might account for Dee shamelessly catcalling the men when they break for lunch and make their way toward the poolside bar. They have to cross directly in front of our little grandstand on their way, and that only encourages Dee to be even louder and more obnoxious as she hoots and hollers for them to "shake it!" and "flex for me baby!" or my favorite, "give momma a spin!"

She truly is ridiculous.

I'm about to take her drink away and convince her to shove some food in her face when an all too familiar deep rumbly voice behind me asks, "Gabriel?"

I freeze, finally understanding what a deer in headlights feels like. I know I should move, should run and hide, should turn and face him, but I'm completely frozen in a mix of terror and disbelief. It can't be him. There's no way... is there?

"Gabriel, that you?" Yep, there is no denying that is my Manu Bennett look-a-like dive instructor, Cade's voice.

Jesus, Mary, Joseph, Sonny, and Cher...

"Yes! That's him! Hi! I'm Deepa, Dee. And who might you be, you tall, dark, gorgeous drink of guava juice?" Dee all but purrs at Cade. Well, that does it. I'm snapped out of my rigor mortis by the need to roll my eyes at that pathetic excuse of a line Dee just fed him.

"Uh, I'm Cade. I took him diving yesterday when my uh... friend had a conflict last minute." Does Cade sound... bashful?! No, no way. There is no way Mr. Self-Assured-Grumpy-Asshole from yesterday is anything but annoyed at having to deal with us lowly peasants in his presence right now.

I finally turn to look at him and let out an involuntary squeak of surprise like a goddamn chew toy. He's standing at the foot of our Bali Bed, still shirtless, wearing only low slung, worn denim jeans with his hands shoved in the pockets and those same reflective aviators from yesterday. He's even more stunning than I remember. Built like a god (seriously, the Manu Bennett description is NOT an exaggeration) with perfectly trimmed stubble tight along his jaw, perfectly full lips that are kissable as fuck but still give him a strong masculine air, and tight cropped black hair I just want to run my hands through.

"So, you're the mystery man my baby Gabriel hasn't been able to shut up about!" I snap my gaze to the traitorous wench, hoping now is the moment I discover my mutant power of laser eyes so I can fry her in half. I have said literally ZERO words to her about him. Slander. Hideous betrayal.

"Is that so? Must have left an impression then," Cade responds.

Was that a smirk? And did he... did he flex?! I think he just flexed. There was a definite movement in his pecs and shoulder region. Not that I'm looking. I... ugh. Screw laser vision. I want the power of invisibility.

"Oh, I think so," Dee coos.

"Well, he dropped to his knees at my feet the moment he saw me, after all." That was most definitely a smirk. Mentally crossing myself, I pray to Madonna for strength.

Dee lets out an unholy squeal of delight and is met with a warm, rich chuckle I can only assume is from Cade. Of course, his laugh would make me melt into a pile of goo. Of course it would.

"Is that so? Well, that's just perfect! He didn't share that little tidbit with me!" she exclaims, slapping me playfully on the arm. All I can do at this point is gape open-mouthed at them and take in their exchange like I'm watching a tennis match.

Cade laughs again, the sound shooting straight through me, settling in my belly, leaving me with a warm feeling spreading through my veins. At least it didn't settle any lower. The last thing I need right now is an unfortunate boner.

"To be fair, it was all a very overwhelming experience for him, even before your fine ass showed up. I kind of abandoned him at the last moment when I came down with something."

"Yeah, my buddy Teo bailed too. Can't say I minded the last-minute dive, though, not when the view was so good." He winked. I know it. He's still wearing his sunglasses, but he absolutely winked. What in the name of all that is holy in Prada is going on right now?

"You know, it's customary for my people to share a meal after experiencing such an adventure togeth-er," Dee explains, and I swear to god she's putting on a Hindi accent as she does. I want to yell at her, '*Bitch, you were born and raised in the suburbs of fucking PORTLAND!*' but my tongue is somehow glued to the roof of my mouth, and I'm incapable of speech.

"Is that so? Well, far be it for me to thumb my nose at your traditions," Cade says with another laugh. I watch as he inclines his head toward Dee in silent question, to which she gives a happy little nod as she wiggles gleefully in her seat. I swear, these two have known each other for all of three point five seconds, and they are already telepathic. Death is too good for her.

Seeing Dee's nod, Cade's lips tug into a slow, sexy grin, and he turns to me. I can see that brow of his rise over the rim of his sunglasses again, an action I've come to see as his signature after being on the receiving end of it several times yesterday. When I take too long to respond to his unasked question, Cade crosses his arms over his chest and asks, "What do you say, Gabriel?"

"He says yes!" Dee answers for me, the girliest giggle I have ever heard leave her face cutting off any chance I had of answering for myself. To his credit, Cade doesn't break his stare, or what I assume is his stare through his shades, waiting for me to speak for myself.

Clearing my throat in an attempt to finally find my voice, I croak out, "I... uh... you don't... I mean... you don't have to..."

Cade's sexy smirk slides into a full-on grin at my response, clearly taking it as the assent he was looking for. "Good. Pick you up in front of the resort at five. Don't be late."

At that, he turns to leave, following his buddies, but stops and twists just his upper body to face me again, lifts his glasses, and gives me a wink before continuing on, disappearing into the crowd by the bar.

I'm dead. I'm dying, he killed me, I'm dead.

Rounding on my friend, my mind screaming at a million miles an hour, the only thing that comes out is, "Please explain to me how a single WINK was somehow the most gratifying sexual experience of my life?!"

"Oh, sweetie. You need better dick," Dee says, obvious sympathy in her voice.

"I do," I nod, settling back against the cushions again and bringing my now melted drink to my lips. "I really, really do."

CHAPTER FOUR

CADE

FROM THE MOMENT I saw him on his knees at my feet on that dock, I knew Gabriel was going to fuck with my carefully planned world. It's been years since I let myself get distracted by a pretty face, or a nice ass, or god forbid a pretty face with a nice ass and the most addictive smile I've ever laid eyes on. Growing up on the island, there was never a shortage of... distractions. I wish I could say I didn't take advantage of that fact and indulge more than my fair share. But let's be honest, I was a horny teenager with very few hang-ups or preferences, so I had my fun and then some. Though four years in the military, straight out of high school, beat that outta me right quick. Some people rankle against the strict rule and order of the military. Me, a wild island child all but raised by the spirits of the island and the waves? I craved it, flourished under it. It made the man I am today.

And that man hasn't let himself fall for a pretty pair of eyes in... Jesus fuck, it's been too long. If Delano and Teo, my roommates, found out it's been damn near a year since I got any real action, I don't even want to think about the Tinder and Grindr parade they would drag through the house to knock me out of it. The sad part is, I don't even have a good reason for having gone this long. It's not like I've been intentionally single or avoiding hookups. I go out with the guys damn near every weekend and have a good time. It's just that no one has caught my eye enough to make me want to take the chance or put in the effort for a night of meaningless sex.

Don't get me wrong, sex is fucking fantastic, but at twenty-nine, I'm kind of over either waking up alone or not knowing (or caring) the name of the person sneaking out of my bed at dawn. Is looking for a connection, a spark, really all that wrong? I didn't think so, but after the last year of looking and not feeling anything even as "electric" as licking a battery... I've started to question things.

Then that crazy little twink fell at my feet on the dock, and I swear, when he looked up at me through those dark lashes of his, lightning struck.

I've never had a preference in my partners really... man, woman, older, younger (within reason), tall, short, curvy, slender, or any color of the rainbow. If I vibed with someone, that was all that mattered. I've never had an answer when someone would ask me what my "type" was in the past. Well, after seeing Gabriel on his knees, looking up at me with that shocked and dazed expression... that. That is my type.

His creamy white skin damn near glowed under the afternoon sun. The only thing breaking up the smooth expanse was a smattering of freckles along his nose and shoulders. His dark lashes fanned over ice-blue eyes so bright I swear they were contacts.

Looking at him, he doesn't fit into any of the classic categories gay men always seem to get shoved into. Kneeling as he was, I couldn't tell how tall he was, but I assumed he was shorter than my six-three frame... Everyone is shorter than I am. Well, everyone other than Siggy, but we don't count the Viking. Regardless of height, Gabriel had one of those frames that no matter how muscled his shoulders and arms may be, he still looked small and compact, like I could toss him around in the bedroom in all the best ways, and he would take it and ask for more.

The thing that really got me, though, was his hair. His shock of silver-white hair captivated and confused me. Looking at his face and eventually hearing him talk, there is no way he is old enough to have gone gray. Still, his stylishly cut hair was undoubtedly silver. I wanted to run my hands through it, tangle my fingers in it while he was on his knees like that, and guide him along my cock. It was even more stunning during the dive. Gabriel and his shining silver hair, a beacon glowing across the reef, begging me to come out and play.

Clearly, I was drugged, or there was some crazy island juju going on because no one, and I mean no one, has ever knocked me this off-kilter before. I called him a fucking "shining beacon," for Christ's sake... if the guys ever heard that shit, I'd never hear the end of it. Yet somehow, it feels right; it feels... like Gabriel.

I've never seen anyone run away so quickly after coming in from a dive as he did yesterday. I could have sworn he had a great time; I'd bet my boat on it, yet he tore down the dock like the hounds of hell were on his heels as soon as I tied the boat off. If I were a betting man, I would have put money on the fact I would never see that little silver shark again. Since none of the usual names fit him, I decided about halfway through the dive to give him my own. As much as he might have been scared shitless to start the dive, he took to it naturally and moved through the water with a sleek grace that I've rarely seen, even with experienced divers. His smooth movements through the water, shining silver hair, and the fact that I didn't see a damn hair on him other than that shock of silver on top solidified him as a shark in my mind. A shark I absolutely wouldn't mind letting take a bite out of me.

So, you can imagine my surprise when he was, lounging by the pool with his loud-mouthed, hilarious spitfire of a friend while the guys and I worked earlier today. We've been working on and off at the resort for a few months now, understanding that the five of us will do whatever random grunt work is needed in exchange for using their pool for dive training and concierges recommending our tours. We get free meals while working and free drinks when we're done, so it's not like we mind having to build a few Bali Beds on the new pool deck.

When I saw Gabriel this morning, or let's be honest, when his friend Dee started yelling at us to "drop it like it's hot" for them, I was more than a little shocked to see him. Thank god for loud, drunk friends because if it weren't for Dee, I don't think I would have recovered from my shock in time to get the date she all but shoved us into. Not that I am complaining one bit.

It may be pathetic of me, a sign it's been entirely too long since I got laid, or that I am still the same horn dog

I was ten years ago. Still, I can't deny the momentary twinge of sadness in my gut when I pulled up to the resort this evening and saw Gabriel standing there fully clothed. Until that moment, I had only ever seen him in... what do you even call those things? The male equivalent of booty shorts? I don't even know, but both times I've seen him, he was in those tiny skin-tight swim shorts that left nothing to the imagination. Seeing him fully clothed almost seems a shame after all that. That doesn't mean he doesn't look great tonight, though.

My initial assessment of him was correct. He's a nerdy type judging by the slim-cut jeans, red chucks, and a t-shirt with chibi Deadpool riding a unicorn on it. Once again, I have discovered my type... Gabriel wearing ridiculous nerdy shit.

I just think Gabriel is my type.

If Gabriel is my type, then my kink is surprising him and getting him to make that little squeaking noise he does when he's not expecting something. I've gotten it a few times tonight and spent more time than I would like to admit trying to get it again. Bringing him out on my boat was the right choice, thankfully. I was a little nervous after how our dive started out; he was so nervous I swear he was vibrating until I got him to jump in the water, but judging by the delighted little squeak and shimmy move he did in his seat when I pulled the car up to the marina, the boat wasn't the issue yesterday. When Gabriel realized my plan was for a sunset cruise and dinner on the boat, you would think I told him Christmas had come early.

"I still can't get over this boat! And it's seriously yours?" Gabriel asks, popping another grape into his mouth. The last of our dinner is packed away, and he's lounging on the large cushioned bench that stretches along the center of the deck between my post at the wheel and the entrance to the small cabin in the bow.

"She was my dad's. I grew up taking her out with him every chance we got. He kept her in storage while I was in the military, and I could finally afford to bring her back out and get her seaworthy again in the last few years. Now I try to get out at least once a week when I can."

"God, If I had a boat like this... and faith I wouldn't knock myself overboard and drown in the first thirty seconds, I would be out every single day." The dreamy look in Gabriel's eyes makes the entire trip out here worth it. He lays back against the cushions, tucking his folded arms beneath his head. Letting him relax a while longer, I busy myself with lowering the sails and dropping the anchor for the night. Or at least, I hope it's for the night.

CHAPTER FIVE
CADE

BY THE TIME I finish getting everything settled for the night, the sun has set, and the real reason I brought him out here is now in full view. Stepping over to where he is still sprawled out on the cushions, I tap his knee, signaling for him to lift his legs. Gabriel lifts his ankles without taking his eyes from the sky, and I slide onto the bench, settling his legs across my lap.

"It's gorgeous out here. I've never seen so many stars." The awe in Gabriel's voice makes this whole night worth it.

"What, they don't have stars back on the mainland?"

"Not like this!" he exclaims, clutching his chest dramatically as he props himself up on one elbow to pin me with a stare. "I'm a city bitch through and through. The only time you get views like this back home is to get out of the city and away from the lights. Now I'll go hiking as much as the next good Pacific Northwestern boy, but you couldn't pay me enough to sleep in those damn woods. No camping equals no stars."

I can't help but laugh at the incredulity in his voice. The death glare he's giving me only makes it better. "City bitch, huh?"

"Fuck yes. At this point, I'm pretty sure my gay ass would shrivel up and die if I lived somewhere without a coffee shop, a salon, and a drag club within a three-block radius," he says, still watching me propped up on an elbow.

"Coffee shop, salon, and drag club? Paints a pretty interesting picture of 'Gabriel at his leisure.' Sounds... like a handful," I say, absently running my hand over his shin, hoping he won't push me away. Thankfully, he gives me a wink and settles back against the cushions, his arms folded behind his head again. The move causes his shirt to ride up slightly, revealing a couple of inches of pale, toned skin.

"Oh honey, if you haven't figured out what a handful I am by now, you might as well bring me back to shore cuz you're in for a rude awakening when this diva gets going," Gabriel laughs, wiggling slightly for emphasis, which only results in him rubbing his ass against my thigh.

"There are so many jokes I could make at that... and none of them are good," I laugh.

"Well, don't hold back on my account," he teases again.

Remember how I said Gabriel on his knees or dressed down is my kink? Yeah. I've changed my mind again. Listening to Gabriel go on and on about his job, things that interest him, and just being... Gabriel, all night over dinner and as we sailed around the island, yeah. That's my kink.

Fuck it, everything about this man does it for me.

He's been driving the conversation since I picked him up tonight, and that's just fine by me. I'm not a man of many words. Maybe my military background makes me more of an observer than one who seeks the center of attention, so letting him take the lead in that aspect is fine. And I know this isn't what he meant when he left me that opening, but it's my turn to take the lead.

Leaning toward him, I brace my hand along the back of the cushions and pause just long enough to raise an eyebrow in challenge. I'm not sure what I expected his reaction to be, but it wasn't what he ended up doing. Reading my move and accepting the challenge in my look, Gabriel gives me a smirk before moving faster than I can follow. Before I can register the action, Gabriel slips one leg from my lap to my other side, wrapping his legs around my waist. Gabriel's look turns decidedly sultry the moment before he reaches up, grabs my jaw in a rough hold, and drags my mouth to his.

There's nothing soft or tentative about this kiss. It's rough and hot and damn near all-consuming. I would never have pegged the spunky little twink to have such an aggressive streak, but I am absolutely here for it. His assertiveness may have caught me off guard, but not being one to get one-upped, I quickly recover and take control of the kiss. Settling more fully over him, slotting my hips against his, I brace my elbows on either side of his shoulders and tangle my fingers in his soft as silk fall of silver hair. Relaxing into my control, Gabriel gives a contented sigh and parts his lips, giving me the opening —literally and figuratively—I need. Slanting my mouth over his, I deepen the kiss, our tongues tangling and fighting for control. Fuck, I need more.

He tastes exactly as sweet as I knew he would, like

sunshine, spice, and hints of the sweet wine we had with dinner. What I intended to be just an exploration, a taste, has moved past that at light speed, and I know I'll never get enough.

I'm not close enough. I need more, need to feel that expanse of perfect skin I saw while diving against mine. Nipping at his lower lip, I pull back and look down at the silver angel glowing in the starlight underneath me. His hands have moved from my jaw to my neck, his fingers toying with the short strands at the nape of my neck. Instead of being annoying or tickling as it has in the past, the sensation only leaves me wanting more... wanting things I haven't wanted in god knows how long. Like waking up, feeling his fingers playing along my skin like that in the morning, teasing me awake with the sunrise.

Gabriel's lips are swollen and red from our kiss, I'm sure, matching my own. His eyes are hooded, his gaze melting me from the inside out as he looks up at me through those dark lashes with nothing but heat and desire burning in their ice-blue depths. At that moment, the nickname I gave him during our dive was never more fitting. My little baby shark wants to eat me alive and fuck if I don't want to let him.

"Inside," I growl, attempting to pull away and sit up. He doesn't release his hold on my neck or waist and ends up moving with me, clinging to me like a damn koala. I have to bite the inside of my cheek to keep from laughing as I look down into his now pouting face, barely maintaining a questioning brow raise in response to his antics.

"What? You think after a kiss like that I'm letting

you go?" he asks, clearly attempting an innocent look, but those 'fuck me' eyes he's sporting give him away.

All I can manage is a questioning hum as he settles more fully in my lap, shamelessly grinding against me while maintaining his pout. If he's not careful, I'm going to bite that damn pouty lip till all he can feel is my mark.

"Oh, Daddy, there is no way in hell either of us is coming up for air before morning," Gabriel says, giving me a salacious wink.

"Daddy, huh?" No one's ever called me Daddy before, and I never thought it would be something I'd be into, but yet again tonight, it's obvious... Gabriel is my kink. I don't care what he calls me as long as I taste those lips again and feel them around my cock.

Gabriel tightens his hold around me and leans in, nipping my bottom lip before dragging his lips along my jaw and to my ear. "Or would your military sensibilities prefer 'Sir'?" he whispers, taking my earlobe between his blunt teeth. I swear I hear a little growl come from him, but for all I know, that was me. Either way, I'm done for.

Sliding my hands under his firm, delicious ass, I grip him tightly as I stand. His lips find my neck as his legs lock tightly around my waist, and I walk toward the open cabin door. Thank Christ, the cabin was the first thing I updated on the boat. Knowing I'd never take her out on long hauls, just short trips around the islands and overnights, I took out much of the living space. Instead, I tucked a king-sized bed into the far end of the cabin in the bow. I navigate the couple of steps down into the cabin as quickly as I dare, with Gabriel and his tongue working their evil magic on my neck, shoulder, and jaw.

I'm barely inside the small space when his hot breath is back on my ear, his tongue teasing the shell as he whispers, "I want that enormous cock I feel grinding against mine deep in my ass tonight. I want you so deep and hard that I can't walk straight for days. Can you do that for me... Sir?" There's a sarcastic lilt to that last word, but fuck if I give a damn. He nips my neck, and my knees go weak. I've never been so turned on in my goddamn life. Taking the last few steps into the cabin and across to the bed, we collapse unceremoniously in a tangle of lips, teeth, and hands onto the bed. Our mouths meet again, fighting for dominance as we tear at each other's clothes. When we are both naked, our hurried movements slow as we explore each other's bodies.

His lean, lithe frame is just as defined as my broader, bulkier one, and I can't stop touching him. I want to run my hands, lips, and tongue over every pale, flawless finger span of that glorious body. Guiding him back against the pillows, I explore his chest, teasing the flat disks of his dusky nipples. The deep groan of satisfaction that rips from somewhere deep in his chest as I torment the tender flesh only fans the flame of my desire. Dragging my tongue across his pecs, toned, if not chiseled, abs, I pause again to place a light kiss below his navel. When I saw him for our dive, I thought he was completely smooth, but now, up close, I can see a trail of silver hairs leading from his navel down past his defined V cut and to his groin. Nuzzling that soft little trail, I drag out the moment a little longer before I lose my mind when my attention finally lands on his cock.

His cock. Fuck. Me.

As if everything about Gabriel wasn't perfect enough, his cock is goddamn beautiful. I can already tell it's going to be my kryptonite. I've always, without fail, been a solid top, but fuck me if I don't want to feel this gorgeous monster tearing me up, ruining me. I must let out a groan, or a whimper, because Gabriel chuckles above me, tearing my attention back to his face.

"Like what you see?" he teases, looking down at me with an indulgent smirk and more than a little pride. The bastard knows he's packing, and fuck yeah, he should be proud. Men would go to war over a cock like that.

Rubbing my slightly stubbled cheek against his hip, I groan as I answer, "Fuck yes. Making me come up with all kinds of ideas for what I want to do with you."

He growls in response and wraps his limbs around me again, attempting to tug me up his body and pull me close. Deciding to let him win this round, I give in and crawl over him, giving in to his kiss. As he kisses me, I moan, our cocks pressing together between us, sending a delicious shock wave through my system. The way they pulse and throb together as we grind into one another is mind-blowing, and if I'm not careful, it will have me blowing my load entirely too quickly.

Letting him control the kiss, I tangle one hand in his hair as I rest on my elbow and let my other hand wander. Trailing my fingers down his side, he lets out a slight giggle as I cross his ribs. Ticklish. I'll be keeping that in mind. I go to tease the spot again, but he closes his teeth around my tongue, not hard, but a clear warning, and I can't help but laugh against the kiss as I drag my fingers lower, leaving him in peace for now. My fingers find the curve of his ass and dig in, dragging a moan from him when the move grinds our cocks together even more firmly.

I need to be inside him. As good as all this feels, I need more. I need to feel his heat surrounding me as I sink into him.

Breaking the kiss, I lean over him, meeting his heated gaze with one of my own. "Hands and knees," I growl, digging my fingers into his hip again.

Gabriel glides his hands from where they were wrapped around my neck, down across my chest, and settles on my hips. He tugs me firmly against him as he presses his pelvis up to meet mine, the friction between our cocks making my eyes roll back as he chuckles darkly. "Oh, Daddy, it's cute how you think you're running this show."

"Is that so?" I ask, leaning in to taste his lips again before reaching into a drawer in the headboard, grabbing a condom and a small bottle of lube.

"Oh, it very much is," Gabriel nods. Without another word, he grabs the condom and lube from my hand, wiggles out from underneath me, and has me sprawled on my back within the space of a blink. I'm about to protest and say I'm not in a receiving mood tonight, but catch myself because for the first time in god knows how long, that isn't exactly true.

Do I want to be inside him more than I want my next breath? Absolutely. But do I have any doubt he would blow my fucking mind with that gorgeous cock of his? Absolutely fucking none.

Some day. But not tonight.

He must read my mind because his smile turns

wicked, and he coos, "Don't worry. I fully intend to have that monster between your legs so deep inside me it rearranges my insides in the next, oh, three-point-five seconds."

"Thank fuuuuu..." I say, but I am cut off when his lips wrap around my cock. There are no tentative licks or teasing tastes, no. This motherfucker takes me to the back of his throat in one suck... and then swallows around my length, taking me even deeper. When his nose brushes along my trimmed pubes and I feel his chin graze my sac, I swear I see stars.

Swallowing around my length one last time, making my vision go white at the edges, he finally pulls back with a self-satisfied hum. When I finally regain control of my vision, it's to the sight of him straddling my hips and rolling the condom down my steely length. Gabriel looks up and meets my gaze, offering me a bright smile before leaning forward and capturing my lips in another searing kiss.

I almost lose myself when I feel the heat of his tight ring against the head of my cock, but thankfully I still retain a sliver of higher brain function, and I grab his hip to stop his descent. "Baby, wait. You need prep," I grit out between clenched teeth.

"Trust me, Daddy; I know what I need. And right now, it's you buried so deep I can't tell where I end and you begin." I go to argue, but he stops me with a twist of his hips that causes the head of my cock to slip past the first tight ring of his entrance. "Fuck, Cade. God, you feel so good. I love the stretch," he gasps as he sinks down another inch, "burns so fucking good."

He gives another twist of his hips, sinking another

inch or two down my length, and that's all it takes to snap the last of my control. With a growl, my hands lock on his hips, and I lift him almost all the way off my length before slamming him down as I arch up, driving him to take me to the hilt. Our cries mingle in the quiet of the cabin as we come together. We both lose ourselves in the punishing rhythm Gabriel sets as he rides me. The slap of his skin meeting mine on each downstroke and the subtle thump of his cock bouncing off my abs as he bottoms out the only other sounds.

I don't know how long he rides me like that, my hands assisting his movements but letting him drive the relentless pace. All I know is entirely too quickly, I feel every muscle in my body tense as I arch my back and dig my fingers into his hip even more firmly. I know he'll have marks in the morning, and fuck if that thought doesn't drive me even higher as I slam him down on me, forcing him to take every fucking centimeter of me before I explode, screaming his name into the void as I release into the condom.

Before the last of my orgasm wracks through me, I hear the telltale sound of flesh on flesh as Gabriel works himself furiously and follows over the edge after me. His release coats my abs and chest, the first spurt reaching as far as my chin. Even as aftershocks continue to rock my system, I can only hold on and watch as the beautiful man above me rides out his pleasure. He's goddamn ethereal like this, his skin and hair glowing in the low light coming in through the small windows, his head thrown back, one arm braced on my knee behind him, and the other grasping his pulsing length as he milks the last of his release from his tip.

This is a sight I could get used to. Something I want to see over and over and know I will never tire of. But fuck me, hearing the way his voice breaks around my name as he comes down, chanting it like a prayer. That. That is the only sound I ever want to hear again.

BRIGHT MORNING LIGHT streams through the small round windows along the bed, rousing me from the best sleep I've had in Cher knows how long. It takes a moment for my surroundings to register fully, but a broad smile pulls at my sleep-stiffened face when they do. The gentle motion of the boat, the ridiculously comfortable bed below me, and, best of all, the solid wall of muscle behind me and the iron band of a firmly muscled arm around my middle.

Cade.

We spent the night on his boat after the absolute best date I have ever been on. When I agreed to go out with him, albeit under extreme duress and pressure from Dee, who I really must buy a fruit basket for or something as a thank you for forcing me to go out with him. I only expected Cade to be a gorgeous face and hopefully decent fuck if we got drunk enough. I never expected him to be the perfect mix of strong, silent type and witty comedian when he wants to be. I can't remember the last time I enjoyed just spending time with someone and talking to them. I swear the man let me prattle on for hours about my job, my life back home, and the stupid things I do to keep entertained in the city. The difference with Cade is I honestly think he was interested in everything I was saying. Most people tolerate my Giant Sparkly Gay Squirrel with Severe ADHD mentality, but Cade seemed genuinely interested in what I had to say, what I do, and what I'm interested in.

Some people might mistake his quiet nature for being aloof or a lack of caring, but even though I've only spent one night with him, I know it's so much more. He's an observer. He listens, learns, and when he has something worthy to say, he doesn't hold back or pull punches. I've met no one like him, beyond being entirely captivating to spend time with,

... Dat Dick Tho...

Oh, sweet baby Jeebus. That dick. That body. That... everything. As much as I adore Madonna, I never understood the song Like a Virgin before... whose dick is so good you feel like you're being touched for the very first time? Cade's dick. That's who. That man has the holy grail of cocks, and I swear to Lady Gaga and all the saints, as soon as I saw it for the first time, the crusty old ghost from Indiana Jones came out and told me I had chosen wisely.

I had hoped to enjoy the warmth of this moment, waking up in Cade's arms for a little while longer, but a rumbling... was that a snarl? Comes from behind me, signaling I have awoken the beast. Or with that giant tentacle between his legs, should I call him the Kraken? Oh! Then I can beg him to release the Kraken! Yep. Kraken it is.

I've awoken the Kraken.

Maybe I can tempt into a round, what would it be, four? Five? Before we head to shore. In an attempt to ease his transition from the dead asleep log he has been since we passed out not long before dawn, I wiggle my ass against him just enough to tease. From the bruises and love bites I can already feel scattered across my hips and rear, I know he was a fan of that particular asset of mine last night.

Cool fingers clamp down on my hip in an iron grasp, startling me as a low growl rumbles through his chest. I can feel the vibration against my back, and I'd be lying if I didn't find it oddly enticing. Pressing further back against him, I wiggle again.

"Sleep," he growls again. Yes, it's definitely a growl. Well, clearly, someone isn't a morning person.

"Come on, grumpy. Time to get up," I urge with yet another wiggle of my ass against his now stiff cock. All I get in response is another low, wordless growl, so I decide to up my game. It's time to sing.

"The sun is up, we're here today, and that's enough..."

"Those aren't even the words to that goddamn horrible song," he grumbles, tugging the hip he still has a hold of and rolling me under him.

"Close enough, and hey, it got you awake, didn't it?"

"I hate Christmas music on a good day. But there is never a good day for that stupid as shit song. And it's especially blasphemous *after* Christmas is over, you heathen."

I could argue, I should argue, but it's hard to argue with the trail of kisses he's leaving along my jaw and neck as he says it.

"Okay, careful there Krampus, you'll scare the children away," I tease before releasing a moan as he sucks on the sensitive spot behind my ear.

"Krampus? What the fuck is that?" he asks, taking my earlobe between his teeth and flicking it with his tongue.

"Krampus. You know, the scary-as-shit counterpart to Santa who punishes and scares all the bad little children on Christmas," I explain, my voice barely more than breathy moans as I force out the words.

"Hmm, punish all the naughty ones on Christmas, huh? You saying you've been bad, baby shark?"

The familiar snick of a cap is the only warning I get before I feel the thick head of his cock probing at my entrance. I try to respond with something witty; I swear I do, but all I manage is a groan as he presses forward, sinking just the tip into me. I may be more than a little sore from last night, but fuck is it worth it and exactly what I want. I quickly lose myself in the slow, torturous pace he sets for us.

I reach for my cock to give myself a little relief from the delicious pressure building within me at his relentless thrusts, but he bats my hand away and takes me in his fist. I'm on the edge of letting go and getting lost in the feeling of him when he starts to hum. At first, I can't place the song, but as he picks up the pace of his thrusts and fist along my length to match the tune, I recognize it.

Oh, hell, nawwwwww.

I scramble to push him off, push him out, get his hand off my length, but he just laughs and starts to sing the lyrics to that god-awful plague they call a children's song. I will give him this; he has a good voice, and that wholly unguarded and gleeful smile damn near steals my breath, but fuck if I will be fucked within an inch of my life while being serenaded by BABY SHARK. No fucking way.

"Get OFF! OMG, you asshole!" I howl, trying my damndest to sound angry, but the more I yell and fight, the harder he's laughing and the louder he sings. It only takes me till the Daddy Shark verse to give in and stop fighting him, devolving into mad giggles of my own. At this point, he's all but screaming the lyrics at the top of his lungs and has started tickling my ribs in that spot he discovered last night.

"Uncle! I cry, Uncle! God! Stop!" I laugh, begging him to stop the torture but not wanting him to stop fucking me. I swear this is the strangest experience of my life, but it's also, without a doubt, my favorite.

"Uncle? I thought I was Daddy last night?" He teases through a blinding smile.

"We've established you're hilarious. We get it. Now shut up and fuck me, Daddy!" I beg.

"With pleasure," he growls, all hints of joking immediately melting away and replaced by smoldering heat.

We spend the next three hours fucking, laughing, cuddling, and fucking some more until we both collapsed after the umpteenth orgasm and snuggle in for a nap. We know we have to return to the real world when we wake up. Still, for a few more precious moments, we both wordlessly agree to spend these last few hours wrapped up in one another in this perfect bubble we have created.

"Sleep, Baby Shark," he mumbles, pressing a sweet kiss to the back of my neck.

"Sweet Dreams, Krampus," I whisper in return. As I drift off into contented sleep, I can't shake the feeling life will never be the same when we wake up. That thought should scare me, but all I can think is that as long as I have Cade's arms around me, I can handle anything.

CHAPTER SEVEN

GABRIEL

I COULD GET USED to this whole 'waking up in Cade's arms' thing. After our epic sex fest last night and this morning... Baby shark fiasco notwithstanding... We quickly passed out again. And now I find myself waking up to the gentle lapping of the waves against the boat's hull and Cade's big, muscular body tangled with mine.

Taking a luxurious stretch, I attempt to untangle my limbs from his and roll toward him. True to his Krampus nature, the big man beside me grumbles in his sleep at my movements. Unable to help myself, I press a soft kiss to the corner of his mouth.

Seriously, my original assessment of him looking like Manu Bennett doesn't even come close to capturing how handsome this man is. And yes, I know we all saw what Manu was working with in a couple of scenes during Spartacus, but seriously, Cade puts him to shame. You'd think after so many rounds I lost count in the last twelve hours, my body would be a little worn out, or you know, ready for a break, but even the thought of Cade's lips on mine has me perking up yet again.

Sliding my hand around his waist, I press another gentle kiss to his lips, hoping to ease him into wakefulness; and maybe tease him into another round. I'm insatiable when the dick is good. Unsurprisingly, Cade merely grumbles and attempts to bat my hand away.

"What are you doing, baby shark?" he grumbles, still mostly asleep.

"Trying to awaken the Kraken," I laugh, kissing him again and pressing my hips closer to his.

With another growl that sounds distinctly more like a groan this time, Cade raises his knees and presses against me, trying to push me away from him so he can fall back into his peaceful slumber.

"Ravenous little shark. Fucking let me sleep," he grumbles incoherently.

I can only chuckle in response, deciding to let him be, knowing I won't win this one. I move to crawl from the bed, but the steely band of Cade's arms snaps out and hooks around my waist, dragging me back into his chest. With several muttered curses, he rearranges us so I'm tucked firmly against his chest, my back to his front once again. He nuzzles his nose into the nape of my neck, pressing a soft kiss there.

"I said let me sleep, not go away," he mutters against my skin, pressing another kiss to my shoulder. Despite his earlier protests and demands for sleep, I feel the unmistakable ridge of his glorious cock pressing against my ass in this position.

So, not as grumpy as he may want me to believe. Liar. I can work with this.

"Oh, is that so? Well, Mr. Grouchy-Grinchey-

Krampus, you certainly didn't sound like you wanted me to stay," I sass, trying to tease him.

"Growly, Grinchey, Krampus? That really the best you can do?" he deadpans, though softening the blow with another kiss to my shoulder.

"Hey, I just woke up. I can't always be perfect."

"I'm seriously starting to doubt that," he breathes, and I can hear the smile in his voice.

"Well, regardless, it's getting late. I wouldn't be surprised if it's afternoon by now, and I'm sure Dee is about to send a search party out after us."

"Unless the search party was shirtless, I doubt Dee would give them the time of day," Cade deadpans. A bubble of laughter escapes my chest, and I press back against him more firmly as I laugh.

"Yeah, you're probably right. The freaking hussy probably hasn't even noticed I'm gone."

"Most likely not," Cade says, pressing yet another kiss to my shoulder, his hands wandering across my waist and hips. My laughter melts into a soft sigh as I enjoy the feel of his fingers trailing along my skin. I'm starting to give in to his lazy ministrations when a loud grumbling gurgle breaks the silence of the cabin.

"Damn, baby shark, you're hungry, aren't you?" he asks, his voice teasing as he grips my hip firmly, holding me still where I hadn't even noticed I had been grinding my ass back into him.

"Hungry for your cock again? Yes," I say firmly, decidedly ignoring the unladylike grumble of my stomach.

"Come on, baby, my cock's not going anywhere. Let's get some actual food in that stomach," Cade laughs, tugging along as he crawls from the bed.

I follow him quickly, trying to locate my abandoned clothes from last night with a huff of annoyance when I notice him strutting confidently toward the stairs and out onto the deck. Buck naked.

"Where you goin' there, Crixus?" I call after him.

He turns to face me, his hands braced on his hips, looking every inch the gladiator I've been fantasizing him to be.

"To get my baby shark food. Where do you think I'm going?"

Bending to snatch the board shorts he was wearing last night from where they lay in a crumpled heap at my feet, I toss them at his head as I say, "Um, forgetting something?"

"What?" he asks with a laugh. "Saying you don't enjoy the view?"

"Oh, I enjoy the view plenty," I say, gesturing towards my groin, where my dick stands, proudly saluting the view in front of me. "I just prefer keeping the view to myself. Thank you very much."

"Getting possessive, are we baby shark?" he teases, his smirk turning devilish.

I sputter in response, only now realizing it is entirely too soon for me to be feeling any level of possessiveness over this man. Even though I'm pretty sure his dick and I are soul mates.

Cade gives a warm laugh at my response and beckons me up onto the deck with him. With tentative steps, I make my way to the doorway, pausing in the middle of the three stairs, unable to fully step out into the sunlight in my birthday suit.

"Calm down, Gabriel. Nothing wrong with you being a little possessive; I quite like seeing my baby shark all jealous. Look around; we got nothing but fish surrounding us. Don't think you have much to worry about. Not to mention I intend to spend the entirety of today naked. With you."

Very few people, and very few things, have ever rendered me speechless. Ever. In my life. I'm pretty sure I can count the number of times I've been at a loss for words on one hand. But this tops them all. Who would have ever guessed the scary-looking cranky man who walked onto that dock to take me diving yesterday would stand here saying such sweet, naughty, horrible, delightful, delicious things to me now?

I'm sure I look like one of the giant fish down on the reef with my mouth working open and closed, trying to find a response to his statement, but nothing comes out.

With another warm chuckle, Cade closes the distance between us and pulls me against his chest, kissing me firmly. He pulls away entirely too soon, and I'm pretty sure I let out a little whimper as his lips leave mine.

"Come on, let's have some lunch and get back to spending our day together. Naked." I wrap my arms around his neck, moving in for another kiss, but he cuts me off with a laugh and says, "Not to mention you look like you could use the sun."

With a laugh, he smacks me on my ass and turns, scurrying away to dig the cooler out from behind the controls where he stashed it last night.

We're munching on the last of our lunch, Cade sprawled out along the cushions of the bench with me leaning against his chest between his legs, when I finally realize I have been chatting nonstop since he dug the food out over an hour ago.

"Okay, I've been talking nonstop since you picked me up yesterday. Your turn."

"What do you want to know?" Cade asks, feeding me a grape.

"Well, other than the fact that you are taking to this whole gladiator role-play thing entirely too well," I say, opening my mouth for yet another grape that he gladly feeds me with a chuckle. "Tell me about you. I know you were in the military, know you grew up here, know about your boat and your dad, but what else do you do? What do you want to do? What makes Cade tick?"

"Oh, so just the lighthearted stuff, got it," Cade laughs, popping another bite into his mouth.

"I'm serious! I told you all about my dead-end job and how absolutely thrilling the whole conference was. Now I want to hear about you."

"Okay, okay. Well, you met Teo, my roommate. We've known each other since we were kids. The two of us, Delano, Siggy, and Jace ran roughshod over the island as kids. Our dads were in the military together, so of course, our mom's all banded together in their own little army wives' posse, which resulted in the five of us being the terrors of the neighborhood and closer than brothers. I won't bore you with our escapades from childhood, but after some of them went off to college and some of us went to the military, somehow, we all ended up back here. Teo and I live in what was his childhood home. His parents left it to him when they passed away five years ago."

I make a soft regretful sound and squeeze his thigh in acknowledgment, not wanting to say anything to break the moment. Cade presses a kiss to the top of my head before continuing.

"It's alright. It was hard at first. Obviously, none of us expected it, but in the end, Teo has always said it was good they went together."

A somber silence settles over us for a few moments, both quietly munching the last of the food. I attempt to impart some measure of comfort through my presence, and Cade quietly absorbs it.

"So Teo and I live in the house, but the other three crash with us more often than not. Honestly, I'm not sure if Sig has his own place. He just couch surfs between the rest of our places," Cade says, his voice returning to the tone I recognize as his standard, controlled persona.

So family is a sore spot. Got it. Not like I don't have plenty of experience with that myself. Before I can comment, Cade continues, offering me another grape between his strong fingers.

"Sig, Jace, and Delano were the other three with Teo and me yesterday working at the resort. The five of us do odd jobs here and there for them in exchange for us using the pool for dive training and referrals for our tours."

"So, is that what you guys do? Give tours to hopeless tourists convinced they're afraid of fish?"

"You're the only client I've had to threaten just to get in the water."

"Hey, your Dom voice is very intimidating," I say, tilting my head back to look at him, hoping he notices the mischievous light in my eyes. His answering smirk and the way his voice has lowered a fraction on his response tells me he did.

"My Dom voice, huh?"

"Oh, hell, yes. My brain shut off, and my body just did whatever you said. No brain involvement required."

"Hm, whatever I say, huh? I like the sound of that," Cade says before capturing my lips in a searing kiss.

I melt into him for a moment, getting lost in the feel of his lips against mine for just a few heartbeats longer before pushing him away.

"Not so fast, Mr. Man. I will not let you distract me that easily; you're not done talking," I say, turning away from him again and snuggling back against his chest.

Cade presses a kiss to my temple, murmuring, "But this is so much more entertaining."

I can't resist pressing back against his kiss, his lips on my skin already becoming my kryptonite

"Maybe so, but I'm not done learning about my Krampus," I say, once again settling back against him and tapping his thigh playfully.

"Alright, alright, so what do you want to know?"

"So, you do the tours and the handyman thing, but do all five of you do the dives? Or are there other things you guys offer?"

"Well, that's the thing. See, Teo and I do the dives, but Siggy and Delano are more of, let's call them, land-based creatures and prefer to give hiking and four-wheeler tours or guided camping trips. And Jace is our mechanic. The five of us would love to start our own tourism company. Do the whole eco-tourism thing. But none of us have a head for numbers, and a bunch of single guys in their 20s aren't exactly the best at saving money. Since I got out of the military, I've been saving up as much as I can, but it's only gotten me so far. I figure I'll have enough capital to put forward in the next two years to get a building and some new equipment so we can make this thing official. Beyond getting all the physical pieces, we should find someone to handle the business side of things. I can muddle my way through with the little bit of business we have now. Still, if we want to expand, I want to find someone with a real head for numbers and business to ensure we're doing everything right."

To an outside observer, Cade may seem like he's just talking about some far-fetched pipedream. Still, I can hear the tone in his voice and feel the tensing of his fingers against my shoulders as he speaks, and I can tell that this is more than that. This is more than just a dream. This is something Cade would fight for and give anything to have. I can't lie; hearing that passion in his voice and the excitement coursing through him almost makes me jealous. I wish I had something I cared about that much, a dream that meant so much to me, and something I would work that hard to achieve.

I must've been quiet for too long because Cade's fingers become a little more insistent as they squeeze my shoulders, and he presses another kiss to my temple.

"What you thinking, baby shark? You got quiet on me."

"No, it's okay. I just... I think that's really awesome. You have a dream, a goal, and it's something you love and are clearly fantastic at. Hell, if you can get my queer ass to not only get in the ocean but enjoy being around all those creepy crawlies, you are clearly excellent at this. And Teo was a great teacher. Fuck, he even got Dee to pay attention for longer than ten minutes. I hope it happens for you. I hope everything comes together and you can see it through because you deserve it. You would be great at it. You all would."

"Why thank you, I hope so too. But why does that make you sound so upset?"

"I'm not upset. I just wish I knew what it felt like to have something you're that passionate about, to have something you care about. I have been coasting for years, and I'm only just now realizing how little I have going on in my life. I'm thirty-three, in a dead-end job I despise, not doing anything even remotely related to my degree. The closest thing I have to a family is that insane bitch I call a best friend and *her* parents."

Cade wraps his arms around my chest, giving me a squeeze, and says, "Now, I'm sure that's not true. I'm sure you have plenty that you love and plenty going on."

"If you had asked me that three weeks ago, I prob- ably would've agreed. But this week, this trip made me realize just how little my life has truly become. I feel like I've been chasing the sunset for years and never gaining any ground, never getting any closer to a goal or anything worth working toward."

"Aw, baby. I know my dick is good, but I didn't think it was *that* good. You don't need to chase it down that hard," Cade says, giving me another squeeze, attempting to break the melancholy mood. I slap at his hand resting on my chest and laugh.

"Shut up, you. Yes, we both know your dick is magic, and if we could, he and I would elope tomorrow. But no, oh modest one, it's more than that. It's seeing people and colleagues, even at the conference, who actually have a passion for this, who have lives they can't wait to get home to. And even Dee, though she bitches about her family to no end, I know deep down she can't wait to get back and see them again. Then there's me, with nothing but a tiny, empty, shitty apartment to go home to and nothing to look forward to other than the snow, which I hate. I don't even have a fucking cat."

"Well, thank fuck for that. I'm deathly allergic."

It's such a simple lie, and it shouldn't make me laugh, but it does. It breaks the tension, and I laugh hysterically until tears stream down my face. I can feel Cade's chest rumbling with his laughter behind me, and for some reason, that just breaks me more. We stay like that, wrapped up in one another, laughing until neither of us can breathe, and our faces hurt from smiling for so long.

As our laughter dies off and we catch our breath again, Cade manhandles me and turns me around so I'm facing him, straddling his lap. His arms settle casually around my waist, and I can't help but mimic the pose, draping my arms around his neck.

He stares at me thoughtfully for a long moment, not moving, not saying anything. The only thing grounding me and keeping me from feeling horribly awkward is the brush of his thumbs against my lower back. Finally, he gives a single nod as if assuring himself of the answer to an unasked question, then leans forward, brushing his nose against the side of mine before whispering,

"You'll find it, baby shark. I know it's out there for you."

CHAPTER EIGHT
GABRIEL

IT WAS ALMOST SUNDOWN by the time we finally returned to the marina. I attempted to help Cade park the boat... tie off? Anchor?... make sure it doesn't float away. Whatever it's called. I don't know, do I look like a sailor? I don't need to know all the lingo to let my own personal gladiator ferry me around on his yacht and feed me grapes while sexing me into a cock coma.

If I had my way, we would have spent another night out there before coming back to the real world. When we finally get back on solid ground, looking at my phone brings me right back down to earth from the high of the last twenty-four hours. I don't have merely a couple of missed calls and texts. Oh, no. Miss Dee, Almighty Queen of the Overdramatic, has called 57 times and texted a conservative 127 times. This is what I get for leaving the most melodramatic attention whore on the planet alone for the night. You would think a grown-ass woman would have something better to do than harass her best friend, who is on a date that SHE SET UP.

I'm just pulling up her contact and ready to dial her when Cade comes up behind me, snaking an arm around my waist and pressing a kiss to the back of my neck.

"You know, if you keep mouthing my neck like that, I'm going to think you're half obsessed with me already," I tease, leaning into his hold. I'm really only half kidding. The man can't seem to keep his lips off my neck and shoulders. He hums contentedly against my skin, nipping gently.

"Nothin' half about it, baby shark," he mumbles, pressing a kiss to my cheek. "But come on, we're gonna be late." His hand slips from my waist as he steps around me but quickly finds my hand, our fingers automatically tangling together like we've done it a thousand times, and he tugs me after him down the dock and toward his car.

"Late? Where are we going? I really should call Dee. She's having an unholy conniption fit," I say, not bothering to disguise my exasperation as my phone buzzes yet again.

"Leave her be. We're not late... yet," Cade says cryptically as he opens the passenger side door for me, waiting for me to climb in.

"You clearly have never met the woman. There is no 'letting her be'... she's more terrifying than a Real Housewife at a sample sale."

"Well, see, now I know you're exaggerating. The Duchess would never be caught dead at a sample sale," Cade says, climbing into the driver's side with a wink.

"Sweet baby Jeebus and all that is holy... he has the Dream Dick—trademark pending—*and* he knows housewives?!" I gasp, pressing the back of my hand to my forehead in a full-on Scarlett O'Hara swoon.

"Trademark pending, huh?"

"Shut up. It's my soul mate. It must be protected," I sniff.

"Protected against all that horrible dick plagiarism. Uh-huh," he deadpans.

"Cock pirates are a very real threat, thank you very much!" I screech indignantly. Clearly, this little moment of teasing has gotten completely away from me, but hell if this queen will ever give in. Cade's rich laughter fills the car's cab as he throws his head back and belly laughs at my ridiculousness.

"Well, I promise to protect my precious cock against any and all evil pirates."

"Damn right, you better," I pout. "And the not-evil ones, too. It's the good ones that sneak up on ya."

Cade reaches across the console and flashes me an indulgent smile as he tangles our fingers together again. "They absolutely do."

A half-hour later, we pull into the driveway of a surprisingly suburban house at the end of a quiet street. All the neighborhood homes are damn near identical—the construction, landscaping, and even the little café sets on all the porches, all perfect copies of one another. The only thing unique about the houses is the color. Four different shades of pastel stucco wash rotate through the houses down the street, clearly the only little bit of customization allowed in this perfect little neighborhood that screams of the 50s military ideal.

"It's so I Love Lucy meets Stepford Wives!" I gush, letting Cade pull me out of the car.

"Told you this is where we grew up. Classic military housing. It's not that bad, though," Cade explains, sounding almost nervous.

I stop him with a hand on his chest. "It's adorable, honestly. I bet it was an awesome place to grow up."

"Yeah," he says, his voice taking on a far-off quality like he's lost in some memory for a moment. "Okay, come on. Now we really *are* late."

THE FACT it took Gabriel until we walked into my house and were bum-rushed by the group of idiots I live with for him to realize he was having dinner with us was rather adorable.

"Bitch! What the fuck are you doing here?!" Gabriel calls, pushing past Siggy and rushing into the living room where Dee is standing, clearly mid-argument with Teo judging by the tension in the room and Jace sitting on the couch with a giddy grin popping popcorn like it's the most entertaining movie he's ever seen.

From any other human, that sentence would sound accusatory and make you brace for a fight. Still, falling from Gabriel's perfectly distractingly pouty lips, I swear it sounds like the sweetest and most endearing reunion you could ever hear outside of a military homecoming.

Dee spins on her heel when she hears Gabriel's screech, a deadly scowl melting into a bright grin at the sight of him. Her smile is warm for all of the two-point-five seconds before her gaze moves down to his neck, and I can see the moment she zeros in on the less-than-subtle mark I left on his collarbone last night. Or was it this morning? Maybe this afternoon? Honestly, I can't keep track and don't care. I like how he looks wearing my mark. So sue me; I never said I wasn't a caveman.

"Who gives a fuck about what I'm doing here!" Dee scoffs, and I can't help but notice Teo square his shoulders and stand straighter at her words. Interesting. I make a mental note to interrogate him about that later. I offer Siggy a chin lift and pat on the shoulder as I walk past and into the house, hearing him chuckle as he shuts the door behind me. The two of us take up positions in the archway to the living space, each leaning against a side of the opening as Dee lays into Gabriel.

"Nope, don't start. I don't want to hear a word from you until you explain that goiter hanging off your neck."

"First of all, that's disgusting, and it's not a goiter. Goiters are nasty ass things old men get. This, my dear, is a love bite. It's an expression of the sweet, sweet loving my soulmate and I shared in the last twenty-four hours," Gabriel explained haughtily.

"Soulmate?!?! He's your soulmate now? Yesterday you couldn't string two words together in front of him!" Dee cackles. I seriously can't keep up with her mood. Is she pissed? Does she think this is funny? I have no fucking clue.

Unable to resist stirring the pot, I interject, "He's talking about my dick."

A chorus of snorts and choked down laughs echo around the room from the guys, and Dee just stares at me while my little baby shark turns a delightful shade of pink. Dee raises an eyebrow at me in question, stepping toward me, and all I give her is a shrug and a smug wink.

"Ohhh, I like him!" Dee declares, all but folding in half with the force of her laughter.

Gabriel rolls his eyes at her outburst and turns around to face me. I can tell he wants to give me hell for saying it, but I give him the same shrug and wink I offered Dee, who is still doubled over with laughter, hands now braced on her knees as she attempts to catch her breath.

"Shut up, you whore," Gabriel huffs, smacking her on her all-but-exposed ass. "You look like a North Pole Hooker. Did you forget Christmas was *weeks* ago?"

To be fair, he's not wrong. The woman is wearing the shortest skirt known to man, and a skin-tight sweater cut so low I'm shocked her tits aren't popping out in her current position. Both are a bright, cheery shade of green with holly embroidered along the edges. To top off the North Pole After Dark look, she has on thigh-high candy-striped stockings, red heels, and a pair of reindeer ears, with her dark hair piled up in two giant buns on top of her head. It's—a lot.

"You can thank that asshole over there for my little getup," she barks, pointing her thumb over her shoulder at Teo, who had clearly been enjoying the view she was giving him a couple of moments ago. "The prick told me it was a Christmas costume thing. I spent half the day tracking all this down!"

"Oh, shut up. I know for a fact you already owned the stockings and the shoes. Though it begs the question of why you brought them on a work trip. Are you wearing the matching garters?"

I swear these two are gonna give me whiplash. In

the span of that one sentence, Gabriel went from exasperated with his friend, his arms crossed over his chest and an unimpressed look on his face, to damn near giddy and smiling, reaching to tug up the side of her skirt and look for himself. Deciding I'd rather not watch him feel up his best friend in my living room, I take a couple of steps to him and tug him back against my chest. I'm surprised when I notice Teo do the same with Dee, an almost territorial glower on his face. Yep, definitely going to call him out on this one later. He whispers something in her ear I can't catch as he pulls her away, smacking her hand away from the side of her skirt where she's still holding it up, showing off half her ass cheek.

"Jesus Fuck, baby shark, you two are seriously going to be the death of me," I rumble against his temple, pressing a kiss there as I wrap my arms around his chest and I walk us back to my spot in the archway, settling him against me.

"You ain't seen nothing yet, Daddy," Gabriel says with more than a hint of teasing pride in his tone. All I can do is growl in response and tug his earlobe between my teeth for a moment.

"Now that the four of you have finished this little pissing match, love fest, lovers quarrel, four-way—thing —can we get on with dinner? The food's getting cold," Delano barks as he stands from his spot on the couch next to Jace, dragging him up to his feet and into the kitchen with him.

"Yeah, yeah. The lovebirds and I will get the table set up. Teo, you and the—what was it? Santa's lady of the night? Whatever. You and Dee get the dishes," Siggy instructs, always the reasonable one of our motley little group. With a round of nods and grumbled agreements, we all dispersed and completed our assigned tasks.

Before I can head out to the backyard to help Siggy with the table, Gabriel turns and presses me back against the wall. "Talk."

"About?" I ask. Honestly, Gabriel, all riled up, really is just too adorable.

"What the fuck is going on?!" he all but screeches.

"You know, you're kinda loud when you're indignant," I tease, leaning in for a quick kiss to the tip of his nose. He smacks my chest and pouts, trying to wiggle away from me, but I keep my arms securely wrapped around his waist.

"I'm not indignant. I'm confused. I have literally zero idea what's going on. As if meeting your friends unexpectedly wasn't terrifying enough, now I have to do it with that ridiculous bitch here too? What is she even doing here?"

"You know, for being your best friend, you two sure sound like you hate each other from the outside," I chuckle, settling my arms more comfortably around his waist.

"It's all in love, I assure you. She's my ride or die. My Spice Girls, if you will."

"Your Spice Girls?" I ask, my brow creasing in confusion.

"Do try to keep up, my dear," he says with a teasing smirk, patting my cheek before settling his palms against my chest. "Yes, Miss Deepa is my Spice Girls—"

At this point, my little baby shark throws his head back and belts out a line or two of *the* Spice Girls' song to demonstrate his point.

"See? Wanna be my lover? Gotta put up with her crazy ass." He smiles up at me, looking entirely too proud of himself for that analogy. "Well, except the whole 'get with' part cuz like—ew."

I throw my head back and laugh, the only real reaction possible to a statement like that.

AFTER SETTING up a long table in the backyard, we all settled in to share the absolutely kick-ass meal Delano made. Fuck me, the man can cook. He may not technically live here, but he knows his way around our kitchen better than Teo and I combined. This is why we keep him around.

Gabriel and Jace helped clear the table after the meal. Now we are all sitting around chatting and enjoying some sort of candy cane cocktail, Dee insisted on making us all. I will give her this; the woman mixes a mean drink. This shit's amazing.

Dee reappears from inside the house, with Siggy close on her heels, a tray of pure heaven in his hands. Before the tray even hits the table, I dive forward and snag a couple of the perfect little treasures.

"Oh Em GEE!!!" Gabriel squeals next to me, and yes, he honestly says the phrase phonetically. I shouldn't find some of the shit he does so damn cute. "What are those?! They are adorable! Almost too cute to eat!" he gushes as he takes a cookie from the tray and inspects it.

"Krumkake. Norwegian Christmas cookies my grandma used to make. I inherited her old iron, roller, and recipe book when she passed because my sister is deadly in the kitchen. Grams taught me how to make them a few years back, and now these heathens demand them as soon as thanksgiving is over. I put a limit at making them past Valentine's, though. Gotta keep something special," Siggy laughs good-naturedly, his deep rumbling guffaw echoing around the small backyard.

"Norwegian? Oh my god you really ARE a Viking!" If I didn't know any better, I would think Gabriel was about to faint from the way he's fanning himself and giving my friend googly eyes. I love Sig to death, but I can't deny the way Gabriel is looking at him makes me put a bit more emphasis on the death side of that equation at the moment.

Because the ridiculous man next to me has, in less than twenty-four hours, gotten so far under my skin and awoken the caveman inside me, I can't resist the urge to reach up and tag the back of his neck, pulling him toward me and growling his ear. "Careful, little baby shark. Keep mooning over Siggy's baked goods like that, and a man could get a complex."

"And we wouldn't want that now, would we?" Gabriel teases, looking up at me with those big puppy dog eyes of his and batting his lashes innocently.

Knowing he won but unwilling to admit it, I simply growl in response and tug him the rest of the way in for a hard kiss. I had intended for it only to be a quick claiming press of his lips against mine, but like everything else when Gabriel is involved, I quickly get lost in the moment, and the kiss goes from quick to claiming with one swipe of his devious tongue. I'm not sure how long we stay lost in each other in the middle of everything, but we are eventually pulled back into the moment by a flying bread roll pegging me in the face. We break apart, Gabriel laughing maniacally and me sputtering and scrambling for the offending roll, ready to toss it back at its owner. I round on the table, ready to fire my pastry missile back at the culprit and find everyone staring with a mix of humor and pleased indulgence at our little display.

"Well, now that you came back up for air, can we please get on with the night? Some of us have things to do, thank you very much," Jace says dramatically, and I know no matter how annoyed he may try to look, there is no heat behind his words.

"Yes, well, don't let me get in the way of your burgeoning social calendar," I laugh, settling my arm along the back of Gabriel's chair and pressing one last quick kiss to his temple before sitting back in my chair, giving my group of asshole friends my full attention once again.

Jace reaches for another bread roll and cocks his arm back, ready to chuck it in my direction again, but Teo stands up and yanks the would-be missile from his fist before he has the chance. Setting it down on the table, Teo turns to address us.

"Calm down, children. Now, if you fuckers are done, I have a little something to say."

Teo, never the one to be serious or make grand declarations in our group, immediately pulls all of our attention when we hear the tone of his voice. We all find our seats again and give him our full attention.

"So, most of you, at least the non-tourists among you, have known Cade and I since before the lot of us could wipe our own asses."

"Not a visual us tourists needed, thank you very much," Dee interjects with a grimace, earning a chuckle from the rest of us.

"Well, it's true, and I wasn't expecting outsiders when I wrote this little speech, so suck it up, woman," Teo admonishes, but I don't miss the indulgent twist of a smile he sends her way.

"Oh shit, he actually wrote a speech! Fuck. He's dying, isn't he?" Delano asks, mock panic painted on his face.

"Don't die on us, Te! Don't die on us, little buddy!" Jace calls out dramatically, clutching his fists to his chest as he pleads up at Teo. We all laugh, and Teo rolls his eyes and smacks Jace upside the head.

"Shut up, you idiot. No, I'm not dying, you assholes. If I was dying, you think I'd tell you at a fancy dinner party?! Fuck you very much. I'm not that big of a dick!"

"Oh, well, that's depressing," Dee sighs, taking a swig of her drink, a perfectly dejected look on her face. Gabriel snorts next to me, and I have to bite the inside of my cheek to keep from laughing out loud. Doing a quick scan of the other three at the table, and I can see they are all fighting back their own laughter at the exchange.

"I didn't—I don't—goddamn you, woman!"

At Teo's bumbling response, everyone at the table loses it, and we all burst out laughing, none of us harder than Dee, who almost snorts wine out of her nose. Never have I seen Teo this unsettled and struggling for words in the twenty-some years I have known him. If I hadn't thought it before, I'm certain something is going on between him and Dee after this brief exchange. My boy just might have met his match in that one. Teo was the biggest ball buster of us all, but something tells me he's got nothing on that woman.

"Jesus Christ. Can we get back to the task at hand, please?" Teo blusters, and I swear I see a bit of a blush staining his cheeks.

"Wait, wait. Did you call this a fancy dinner party? Who invited the stripper to a fancy dinner? Is that a thing? Have I been missing out?" Jace heckles again just as we catch our breath. Of course, that sets us all off again, with Dee and Teo both smacking Jace upside the head in retaliation.

"Uncultured swine, the lot of ya. Seriously. Can we *please* get back to it now?" Teo pleads, trying again to get us hooligans under control.

"Sorry man, yes, you and your enormous wang can continue with your death announcement," I say, rolling my hand in front of me, signaling him to move on.

"Thank you. My gigantic cock and I will do just that," he says, sounding entirely too smug for someone who just needed one of his buddies to reaffirm the size of his dick.

"You're kind of an idiot; you know that?" Dee asks, looking up at him with a sweet, if slightly confused, smile.

My attention is drawn away from the strange level of non-sexual sexual tension flowing between those two by Gabriel gripping my thigh tightly with a gasp.

Turning to look at him, I see he's staring wide-eyed and slack-jawed at his friend at the other end of the table.

"Well, slap my ass and call me Liza. She's doing it!" he whispers, with no small amount of awe in his voice.

"Doing what?"

"My cold-hearted, cranky, bitchy witch of a best friend is flirting!"

"Babe, from what I've seen, Dee would flirt with anything male that has a pulse. Are you forgetting yesterday afternoon by the pool?" I ask, wondering what has him so shocked.

"No, no, no, shut up. There is a *huge* difference between flirting and *flirting*. I have known Miss Priss for years and have never once seen her come anywhere within the same galaxy as actually *flirting* with someone." Gabriel finally tears his eyes from the other end of the table and turns to me. "What in the name of Bette Midler is in the water down here? Do all of you have magic cocks or something?"

"Dude, say that a little louder; I don't think they heard you down on the beach!" I cringe at Siggy's laughing admonishment, bracing for Gabriel's inevitable embarrassed rambling retraction, but Siggy heads him off. "Pretty sure I am all for a ringing endorsement like that spreading around. I can just picture the line at our door waiting for a chance at our magic dicks!"

"I give up," Teo huffs from the end of the table, sitting down and throwing back the rest of his beer in one gulp.

"Okay, okay, I'm sorry, man. We'll behave. Finish what you were saying," I say, attempting to get my laugh under control.

"Nope, you fuckers ruined it. Here," he gripes, throwing an envelope toward me, and landing it in the middle of the table. "Surprise, dickheads." With that, he flops back into his seat and takes a long pull from a new beer bottle Dee magically materializes in front of him.

With a snort of derision at his antics, I reach for the envelope and tear it open. Inside is a single folded piece of paper. Scanning it quickly, my heart races, and I read it over at least three more times to ensure I am reading this correctly. I look up in confusion and meet Teo's grin.

"How?" is all I can manage to ask.

Teo just shrugs and lifts his beer toward me in a salute.

"You are the worst at this! What's it say?" Gabriel reaches for the paper I'm still clutching in my fists, my brain still not fully comprehending it.

"Share with the class, man!" Jace calls from across the table as Gabriel scans the sheet.

"Oh my god! It's a business license! Honu Adventures LLC."

A chorus of cheers sounds around the table as the rest of the guys realize what that means. Teo did it. He started our company. The dream we've had for as long as I can remember is finally coming true.

"But how? We still don't have the money," I finally ask.

Teo shrugs again, "Remember that call I got a few weeks back from that lawyer on the mainland? Apparently, I had some rich uncle who croaked with no other living family and no will—so—happy random inheritance to me?"

My mind is racing a million miles a minute trying to

process all this. If Teo is serious, we have it. We have the company; we have the money; we have the manpower—we could actually make a go of this, and soon. I know I should be overjoyed, and I am really, but something is nagging at the back of my mind that I can't seem to shake. There's this feeling that something is missing that would make this moment perfect, making the thought of starting this new venture much more amazing.

It really should terrify me more than it does when I realize I think that missing element, that missing part of the equation—is Gabriel.

CHAPTER ELEVEN

GABRIEL

A FEW HOURS LATER, the sun has set, and Dee and I are sitting on the back deck of the guy's house, sipping yet another round of candy cane cocktails. The boys all ran off inside as soon as dinner was cleaned up and started making plans for their new company, now that it was officially moved from dream to reality. It's like an honest to god little Orphan Annie moment, and fuck me if I don't want to sing about tomorrow being only a day away.

"Sing, and I'll cut your dick off," Dee casually threatens, pulling my attention back to her. I must have been lost in thought again from staring off toward the beach I can barely make out in the distance through the trees.

"How did you know?!" I ask with an incredulous scowl.

"Queer, please. You think I don't know the face you make when you're about to go full Broadway on me?"

I grab a chunk of candy cane off the side table between us and lob it at her in retribution for her sacrilege. "More often than not, you join me when I go full Broadway, and you know it, you twat!"

"That's beside the point. And anyway, you were talking to yourself again. I would love to hear you explain how a dead uncle is the same as a rich Daddy showing up and saving you from a drunk Carol Burnett."

"You can't tell me you wouldn't love being raised by Carol Burnett, Tim Curry, and Bernadette Peters. Come on. A trio of the gin-soaked gods right there."

"Stop changing the subject," she snaps.

"What exactly *is* the subject?"

"What you're going to do about your little soulmate problem. And don't even try to argue with me that he's not, or you don't believe in that shit. We both know it's true so let's move past the denial phase and into the problem-solving, so you can have your happily ever after, shall we?" she says with a haughty wave of her hand as if dismissing my concerns and opinions before I can get a word in.

"What is there *to* do? He lives here and has a life here. Hell, as of about an hour ago, he has a business here. I live back home. I have you, my job, and my apartment, and you know Mama Suman would kill me if I even attempted to leave her without a canasta partner." My excuses sound weak, even to my own ears, and I don't believe them even as I say them.

If I'm honest with myself, I have been trying to come up with reasons or justification for why I need to stay away and why I need to go home since we left the boat this afternoon... and I'm struggling to find many. I all but admitted I have no life to Cade last night, and while it was embarrassing to admit, it was also a bit of a wake up call to realize just how little I have tying me down back home. Hell, even calling it home is a stretch.

I have Deepa and her family, who have all but adopted me and accepted me as one of their own, but outside of them, there is very little to go home to. I have a shitty apartment, an even shittier job, and absolutely no prospects for changing the trajectory my sad life has been on for god knows how long. Wow, that's a fucking depressing thought.

"Nope, not doing that either," Deepa says, breaking through the melancholy fog of my thoughts and dragging me back to the present. "We aren't doing the denial or the pity party thing tonight. We are both more fabulous than that, and the brooding, depressed look doesn't suit you, babe."

"You're so sweet," I grumble, taking another sip of my drink, more for something to do than anything else.

"You know I'm right. You are trying to convince yourself you don't deserve this. And I will not stand for that bullshit. You hate your apartment, I'm not even going to mention the dead-end jobs we both despise, and my freaking mother can find a new partner for cards. You deserve to be happy, babe."

I open my mouth to argue, but she cuts me off again.

"I mean it. You, more than anyone I know, deserve to be happy, to take a chance on yourself, and see that there is more in life for you. You've done it once before and found out there was so much more than that abusive, judgemental, stuck-in-the-fifties, backwater bullshit town you grew up in and found a place where you could grow into the amazing sarcastic asshole ray of sunshine I know and love."

"Well... damn," is all I can manage to get out around the lump in my throat as I furiously try to blink back the tears threatening to fall. I don't cry. I don't. And I refuse to let this bitch be the one to bring it out in me. Nope. Not going to happen.

"Gabriel, I know we are a pair of catty bitches most days, and you know I would do anything for you. I adore you and only want the best of you."

"And what do you think is best for me? Because right now, I feel like there is no winning," I say with a sigh.

"I can't tell you what is best, only that all I want is for you to be happy. So tell me this, could you see yourself here? See yourself being happy here? Even with or without Loverboy?"

And that's the million-dollar question, isn't it? Do I even really know what happiness looks like at this point? Sure, I am a generally happy person. You can't be as fabulous as I am on a day-to-day basis if you are consistently miserable. But am I truly happy, like deep down on a real, meaningful level happy? I don't know if I ever have been or what that truly means. How depressing is that?

With that wholly depressing realization settling around my shoulders like a wet blanket, I take a moment to consider Deepa's question. Could I see myself happy here? With Cade? If the last two days are anything to go by, the quick answer is obviously yes. I don't think I have had that much fun in and out of bed with someone, maybe ever. He makes me laugh, makes me think and feel, and gives me the best orgasms in living memory. But that is all surface level. What about the rest of it? Can I see myself here, on the island, being happy with or without Cade?

The speed with which the answer comes to me is almost shocking.

"Yes. I can see myself here. I can't..." but Dee cuts me off before I finish my thought.

"No. I don't need to hear more. You said yes; that's all that matters. And for what it's worth, I can see you here too. I haven't seen you this relaxed, just yourself, in I can't remember how long. Do you even realize you haven't had that damn frustration crease in your forehead since we landed? Even during the conference, you were more chill than you ever are back home. The island looks good on you, babe," Dee says with a soft smile. "So, now the question is, why don't you do it? Give me one concrete reason you shouldn't take the plunge."

"Honestly? I don't have one. I don't know." And isn't that just the kicker?

A throat clearing behind us draws my attention and we both turn to see Cade standing in the open patio doorway. "Uh, hey. Sorry, didn't mean to interrupt but didn't want to eavesdrop like a creeper either."

"I ain't been droppin' no eaves, sir, promise!" Teo calls from over Cade's shoulder, pulling a barking laugh from me, a blank unimpressed look from Deepa, and an eye roll with an elbow to the gut from Cade.

"Aaaaand, that's my cue. I'll leave you two to it and take the fool of a took with me," Dee says as she stands and brushes past Cade, grabbing Teo by the ear and dragging him back inside behind her.

Cade and I watch the pair disappear into the house for another moment before he turns to me with a shockingly shy smile. Seeing such a timid expression on his usually self-assured features is damn unsettling. Someone as gorgeous as him, someone so full of life, should never look that upset. Grumpy, sure, but he's a loveable grump. It's all part of his charm.

"So…" I drag out, suddenly horribly awkward now that we are alone. I stare out over the backyard and through the trees and can just make out the sun setting over the waves. Those damn sunsets again.

"Yeah, so… I, uh…" Cade stammers. He's clearly just as lost for words as I am at this moment. His hands are clasped awkwardly in front of him as he rocks slightly back and forth on his feet.

Well, isn't this reassuring of our future prospects?

"I'm sorry I was listening…"

"I'm sorry about what I said…"

We both say, talking over one another as we turn to face each other. Our eyes go wide with matching expressions, clearly not expecting the other one to say what they did.

"Sorry, you go first," I say, waving a hand wildly toward him. I swear this level of awkwardness is not healthy. I lose all control of my limbs and mouth when the tension gets this high. So not good.

"No, you go. I'm sorry," he concedes with a polite, almost indulgent smile before nodding toward the chairs Dee and I had occupied a few moments ago.

With a sigh, I nod and turn to reclaim my seat, taking a moment to get my racing thoughts in some semblance of order. Once we are both settled and I can feel his eyes on me again, I take one last deep breath before turning to face him fully.

"I'm sorry for what I said. What I assume you overheard. I don't want things to be awkward or for you to feel like I am making more of this than what it is. You have given me no reason to think this is more than just a vacation fling. Hell, for all I know, this is your standard M.O. for dealing with tourists. To be honest, I wouldn't blame you one bit! That's a pretty sweet setup, honestly. Let all the random mainlanders fall right in your lap! Wow, I can't believe I hadn't thought of that before..."

"Gabe. Stop," Cade's loud admonishment cuts through my ramblings, but the warm hand he presses to my thigh before squeezing gently brings my runaway mouth to a screeching halt. See? Awkwardness is dangerous.

I stare back at him in what I can only assume is a deer in headlights look before he gives me another one of those soft smiles and continues.

"First things first, no. Picking up random tourists is the furthest thing from my usual M.O. In all honesty, I can't remember the last time I hooked up before you got here. That's just not how I work. But more importantly, you didn't make anything awkward. Well, the last few minutes excluded," he says with a teasing wink that only makes me blush. "You're right. I haven't said anything about what this is, or let us talk about anything past your vacation. I wanted to enjoy our time together for what it was and not let anything bring us down. I overheard a bit of what you and Dee were talking about. I'm sorry again about that. I hadn't meant to listen in to a private conversation."

"It's fine. It's your house anyway," I rush to assure him, once again interrupting him.

"Gabe, what I am trying to say is... well, what if you

had a reason to stay?"

The question falls from his lips with so much earnest sincerity, it all but takes my breath away. His hand, still resting on my thigh, gives a gentle squeeze again before rubbing lightly back and forth in a comforting motion, but one clearly meant to drive home the fact that he is here, with me, in this moment.

Stay? Could I really stay?

"But... what would I do? Where would I stay? I just... how?"

"Obviously, we would have to figure things out, but thanks to Teo, we have a business that needs running, and from what I have heard, you have quite the head for numbers and spreadsheets and shit. The lot of us are nightmares with the business side and could absolutely use someone with a good head on their shoulders to help keep us in line," he says with a chuckle. He's not wrong. After meeting the rest of his friends, the thought of the five of them handling the business side of anything makes a shudder run down my spine.

"So what, I would be? Your employee? Where would I stay? Would there be enough for me to do to make rent and pay bills and all that shit? What would I be?" I can feel myself spiraling; it must show on my face because Cade's hand reaches for me and tugs me back. I hadn't even realized I had stood from my seat and was pacing in my near panic. Staring back at him, sheer panic and confusion written all over my face, I watch as he stands from his seat and closes the distance between us. With a small smile, he lifts both hands to cup my neck, his thumbs grazing my cheeks with such tender affection it stops my breath in my chest.

"You'd be mine. Full stop. Just mine."

CHAPTER TWELVE

CADE

I CAN'T SAY for certain if I had fully intended on asking him to stay when I stepped out onto the back porch a few minutes ago, but hearing Gabe and Dee talk about the life he has waiting for him and how discontented he is there, it just broke something in me. The idea of asking him to stay has been rolling around my mind since yesterday, or maybe even since that first dive, if I am completely honest. But regardless of when the idea took root, now that it is out in the world and I am staring down into the surprised ice-blue eyes that have come to mean entirely too much to me over the last week, I can't deny it feels... right.

All of this feels right. Gabe, Dee, because let's face it, those two are a package deal whether they want to admit it or not; where one of them goes, the other is sure to follow before too long. But the thought of both of them running around here and having Gabe help get the business off the ground sounds... perfect.

I can see the gears turning in Gabriel's head as he processes what I just said, and I brace myself for a thousand different arguments and excuses. I know it's fast and maybe more than a little crazy, but I also know we can make it work. Whatever the issues or roadblocks, I know we can make it through. He's worth it, and this thing between us, however tentative it might be right now, feels worth it.

"But, but I have to leave tomorrow. We have tickets, and my job is expecting me back, and my apartment, and..."

I can see the panic mounting behind his eyes and cut him off with a kiss, needing to bring a halt to the runaway train that I'm learning his thoughts can easily turn into. At the press of my lips against his, Gabriel sinks into me, giving over to the kiss immediately. What I had intended to be only a quick press of my lips to his quickly becomes heated when he opens for me, all but begging for me to take more control. Unable to resist stealing a taste of him, I sweep my tongue into his mouth, tangling with his and groan at the sweet, minty burst of him.

With a sigh, Gabriel goes completely limp against me, giving me all of his slight weight, surrendering to the kiss, to me. My arms come around him without a second thought, one hand cupping the back of his neck and the other arm banding around the small of his back, crushing him against me.

"Give me tonight. Just tonight. Let us have one more night together before we have to make any decisions. One more night before the real world closes in," I all but plead when we break to come up for air.

Gabriel's eyes slowly drift open and meet mine, a dazed kiss-drunk haze clouding those usually razor-sharp icy blues. He searches my face for a moment before his gaze slides past me toward the yard and the sun that is quickly sinking below the waves in the distance.

"One more sunset." I can hardly hear his mumbled words, but I know their significance to him. Unwilling to let him fall into a spiral of darker thoughts again, I nudge along his jaw with my nose, nipping and teasing as I go to distract him.

"One more night. Let's go to your hotel and lock out the rest of the world while we still can," I tempt against his ear, teasing the tender lobe with my teeth. Gabriel shudders in my arms and only manages a little whimper and a nod before turning to meet my lips again.

Before we can get too distracted again, I pull back and urge, "Let's wrap up here and head out before it gets too late."

"Eager much, Daddy?" Gabriel teases, a hint of the sass I expect from him finally coming back.

Grabbing his hips, I tug him closer, pressing him against the prominent bulge in my shorts. "You have no idea how eager, baby shark."

That earns me a groaning laugh and a heavy eye roll as Gabriel shoves away from me. "Don't you *dare* start singing, or there is no way I am letting you come back to my room with me."

"You sure about that?" I say against his ear, dropping my voice to a sexy growl as I pass, heading into the house.

I hear him groan loudly behind me and call, "not fair!" just before I step through the back door of my house once again.

• • •

After a string of entirely too many goodbyes, assurances there would be no late-night elopements, and plenty of catcalling and less-than-subtle innuendo, Gabriel and I finally made it out to my car and to his hotel. It was a quiet drive, neither of us sure what to say, but saved from too much awkwardness from the wind whipping through the cab of my jeep since I still had the roof off. The only thing keeping me from second guessing our plans for the night was the death grip Gabe kept on my hand the entire drive, like he was afraid to let go, that I might disappear... or he would... if our connection broke.

Any amount of mischief we might have gotten into on the elevator ride up was thwarted by an older couple who entered the cab with us, explaining the entire ride to Gabriel's floor how they were here for their 40th anniversary and how we just *must* go to the luau the hotel hosts. Unlikely.

When we reached his room, the tension was heavy in the air, hanging between us like a wall neither of us could quite see over. Gabriel looked around the room nervously, his fingers twitching at his sides as his teeth raked over his lower lip. "Well... um..."

Unable to stand the horrible awkwardness a moment longer, I stepped forward, closed the gap between us, and tugged the abused flesh of his lip from between his teeth with my thumb, ducking my head slightly to meet his gaze. At the touch of my finger, he let out a groan I am pretty sure the old couple three floors up could hear, and I did the only logical thing that came to mind. I shoved my tongue down his throat to keep him quiet. Thankfully, Gabriel took the hint and melted against me, any tension from a moment before clearly long forgotten as we both lost ourselves in the kiss.

Pulling him closer, I tilt my hips, aligning our groins together. The feeling of grinding against him shouldn't be as mind-blowing as it currently is to feel his increasingly hard length against mine, even while both are still trapped in our clothing. Gabriel doesn't stay passive for long, though. His greedy fingers are quickly tugging at my clothing, pulling at the hem of my shirt, tugging on the laces of my shorts, making no progress on a particular item before moving on as our kiss gets more and more desperate.

"Patience, baby shark." I grin against his lips as he growls at me, nipping at my bottom lip as he once again tugs at my shirt, attempting to rip it from my body, but I refuse to lift my arms and help him; they are entirely too happy where they are at circling him and holding him close. Wanting to distract him from his efforts, I slide my hands into the back of his shorts, grabbing handfuls of his perfect bubble butt and using my hold to drag him even closer. His head falls back on his shoulders with a long groan as he leans into the move, grinding himself shamelessly against me.

"Please," he all but pants as he meets my kiss once again, finally giving up his desperate attempt to undress me and instead slipping his hands under the fabric of my shirt and exploring my chest and abs. When his fingers graze the tight disks of my nipples, I groan, tangling my tongue with his.

Pulling back from him is a colossal effort at this moment, but I have my sights set on a bigger reward. With an almost pained whimper from him, I step out of his hold and let my gaze rake over him, from the flush of his cheeks to the tips of his toes.

"As much as I love that hot look in your eyes, I would much rather feel those hot hands or, even better, that scorching cock of yours. Get back here!" Gabe demands with a sultry little pout that only makes me chuckle. "Oh, that evil laugh... do it again." The blissed-out look that crosses Gabe's face is enough to make me do just that, and I chuckle darkly as I reach for his shirt and tug it over his head in one swift move. Before he can say anything else to distract me, I have his pants and those sinfully tight briefs falling around his ankles.

I had so many plans and things I wanted to do to him tonight, but I don't care about any of them now. All I care about is the absolute perfection standing tall and desperate, with a sweet little bead of pre-cum already kissing the tip, between Gabriel's thighs. Stepping backward, I wrap my hand around his straining length and use my hold on him to guide him with me. At the first touch of my hand around him, Gabe lets out a sigh as his eyes roll back and drift closed until he realizes what my intentions are, and he breaks into a strangled laugh while I continue to tug him along with me until my knees hit the edge of the bed and I sit. I give him a slow stroke from root to tip while meeting his gaze before offering him a wink as I lean forward and take him into my throat in one swift move.

The first burst of his pre-cum hitting my tongue has me groaning, and any thought of subtlety or taking it slow flies from my mind. He's everything. Sweet and salt, light and warmth, everything I never knew I wanted and am now terrified to lose. Both are sobering and terrifying thoughts for someone who only a few days ago had thought they knew their path, who they were, and what they wanted. But this little silver shark swam into my life and proved just how wrong I was. The scariest part, I can't say I would have it any other way.

Pushing all other thoughts from my mind, I focus on my task, on this moment, and the incredible man with the delicious cock before me. With that thought and only that thought in my mind, I circle his crown with the tip of my tongue before swallowing him down again. Gabriel's breath catches above me, and I swear it's the sweetest sound I have ever heard. He lets me set the pace, my hands alternating between guiding his hips and exploring the expanse of soft skin now open to me.

My fingers reach his crease to tease him when there is a knock at the door, pulling my concentration from my task. I move to pull away, but Gabriel tangles his fingers in my hair, trying to hold me against him. With a chuckle, I press a quick kiss to the tip of his cock, unable to resist swiping at the little bead of sweetness that rises to greet me before I push him to step back and allow me to stand.

"I'll be right back. Don't you dare move, baby shark," I growl against his ear as I slip past him, snagging my shorts and tugging them back on as I make my way to the door. Tucking myself back in and zipping up again is not the easiest nor most comfortable thing I have ever done, but I get myself mostly presentable before I open the door and find... nothing on the other side.

Biting back my annoyance, I lean out into the hall and look one way and then the other, trying to see who knocked so I can lay into them about interrupting a man while he's eating his favorite meal, but my toe catches on something cold. I look down and find a bottle of champagne on the carpet with a post-it note stuck to the side.

Hydration is key.
~Auntie D

I can't help the snort as I pick up the bottle and see the Costco-sized tube of lube hiding behind it. Grabbing up the champagne and pocketing the lube, I turn back into the room, letting the door swing shut behind me with a resounding thud. The sight I'm greeted with has me forgetting the bottle now hanging limply at my side. Gabriel is laid out across the middle of the bed, one hand thrown casually behind his head, the other wrapped around his cock, stroking himself in lazy pulls, his legs spread, giving me just the barest teasing glimpse of where I so desperately want to be.

Giving myself one more moment to take in the utter perfection that is the man before me, I take another lazy sweep of his form with my eyes before I clear my throat and clamp down on the desire raging through my veins like liquid fire. I am not ready to relinquish the upper hand just yet, so I use the distraction of opening the bottle, taking those few moments to compose myself.

"Whatcha got there?" Gabriel asks, his voice dripping with heat and desire as he continues stroking himself lazily.

"Auntie D sends her love," I chuckle, lifting the bottle a little higher for him to see before popping the cork and wrapping my lips around it to catch the little bit of fizzy overflow.

"If she really wanted to convey her love, the bitch should have sent lube," he sasses, spreading his legs suggestively.

"Oh, she did that too," I say with a wink, pulling the tube from my pocket and tossing it onto the bed next to Gabriel's hip.

"She does love us!" he cackles, and I can't help but laugh along. The two of them truly are ridiculous, but I can't deny the fierce devotion and love they share, even if it doesn't make much sense to an outside observer.

"Well, since it's here, I figure we should celebrate," I say, taking another swallow directly from the bottle.

"Celebrate? And what exactly are we celebrating?" Gabriel asks, releasing his cock finally and propping himself up on his elbows, meeting my eyes more fully.

"Well, the way I see it, regardless of what happens in the morning, tonight we are either sending you off with a bang after one hell of a vacation... or we're celebrating the start of a new journey. Either way, I think it deserves to be commemorated."

"Sending me off with a bang, huh?" he teases, raising an eyebrow at me.

"Oh, you know that's a given tonight, baby shark," I say with a wink before taking another swig.

"I warned you once already. Don't you dare start singing again, Daddy!" he all but screeches, scrambling up to his knees. I am pretty sure he is attempting to look intimidating with his hands on his hips and a challenging eyebrow raise, but his still hard cock straining toward me, bobbing slightly from his movements, really kind of ruins the effect. Not that I would ever dare tell him that.

Instead, I decide to close the distance between us, crossing to the side of the bed at a leisurely pace. "What?" I ask, leaning toward him in the center of the bed, the hand not holding the bottle bracing my weight against the mattress. "I thought you liked my voice?" I all but purr against his ear.

A full-body shiver skitters down Gabriel's spine, and he audibly tries to swallow a groan before he grinds out, "when it's doing that gravelly growl thing in my ear as you sink balls deep in my ass? Fuck yes, I love your voice. When you sing the devil's song and torture me? Not so much."

"Ah," I growl against the sensitive spot just behind his ear. "Good to know."

Gabriel moans as another shiver runs down his spine, his skin breaking out in goosebumps. He turns his head, attempting to catch my lips. I pull back with a grin before he connects, raising the bottle between us as his lower lip juts out in the most adorable and pathetic pout I have ever seen on a grown man.

"To us, to tonight, and whatever happens next," I say, lifting the bottle in a toast. Gabe reaches for it, but I ignore his outstretched hand and bring the bottle to his lips, tipping it up for him to drink. To his credit, he swallows most of what I offer, but a trickle of the sweet liquid slips from the corner of his mouth and down his chin before I can pull the bottle away. Again, before he can take care of it himself, I lean in and catch the drop with the tip of my tongue, dragging it back up the path to his mouth. The gasp Gabriel lets out as our lips connect is the sweetest sound, one I fully intend to hear as often as possible tonight. Deepening the kiss, I sweep my tongue past Gabriel's parted lips and lose myself to his taste, the sweet combination of the champagne and something uniquely Gabe.

Before I lose all sense of my plan for the night, I pull back, grinning at the kiss-drunk glaze in Gabriel's eyes. He blinks up at me a few times, a soft smile on his kiss-swollen lips before he seems to regain some hold of his senses and looks questioningly back at me. "What about you?"

"Needed a taste of you first."

An adorable blush blooms over his cheeks and crawls down toward his collarbones as I lean in closer, my proximity pushing him back against the pillows until he is lying almost flat again.

"My turn," I say, a slow grin spreading over my features as I lift the bottle again.

CHAPTER THIRTEEN
CADE

THE EARLY MORNING sun falling across the bed pulls me from a deep, exhausted sleep. I lost track of how many times Gabriel and I came last night, and by the time we finally passed out, tangled around each other, I was so spent I slipped under almost immediately. My body is sore in the most delicious ways, and I am in no way ready to join the land of the living. Rolling away from the window with a pained groan, I reach across the bed for Gabriel, wanting to pull him against me again. When I stretch my arm across the pillows, I don't meet the warmth of Gabriel's skin like I was expecting, instead; I find nothing but cool rumpled sheets.

Finally cracking an eye open, I look over at his spot and find it empty. I want to believe he is just in the bathroom or grabbing a drink, but the cool sheets tell me he's been gone for a while. Maybe he's just sitting out on the balcony? Or the couch? Anxiety before a flight is a thing, right? Maybe he just couldn't sleep.

I know it's all bullshit, but I refuse to accept the

reality I know is waiting for me if I look around the room. Gabe is gone. My little baby shark slipped out sometime after our night together and took off.

This shouldn't be such a surprise. I knew he had a flight today and was leaving, regardless of how much I wished he would stay. Even if he wanted to stay with me, there are things that need to be taken care of back home for him. No one can leave on vacation and just disappear. That's not how the world works.

Despite wanting to ignore reality as long as possible, I know I will never be able to get back to sleep now, so I might as well face whatever is waiting for me outside the cocoon of these blankets. With a deep, centering breath, I brace myself for the inevitable and pull the blankets away from my head. Sitting up, I look around the hotel room.

Knowing he would be gone and seeing the empty room are two very different things. I can't help but get up and look in the closet for his bag, stick my head into the bathroom and check the counter for the handful of products that had been scattered there last night. It's all gone.

I don't know what hurts more, knowing he left without waking me up for a goodbye, which, if I'm honest with myself, I didn't really expect anyway, or that after my quick check of the room, I don't see a note, or even so much as a business card with his number on it left for me. In the span of a couple of hours, Gabriel went from a tangled, sweaty, panting, beautiful mess in my arms to nothing more than a passing memory.

As I gather my clothing, still scattered around the room from where it was tossed last night, the inevitability of my current situation increasingly grates on my nerves. By the time I am tugging on my shorts, my melancholy has morphed into barely contained anger bordering entirely too close to rage or my liking. My hip screams in protest as I trip over one of my shoes and crash against the dresser. The urge to throw something is nearly overwhelming until I catch sight of myself in the mirror.

"Perfect," I grumble, scrubbing at a mark on my chest. Gabriel leaves without a trace, no note, not even a sock left under a chair. He left me with nothing to remember him by, except a damn hickey. The sentimental part of my heart, the part I have been trying my damndest to keep quiet since he stumbled into my life, wants to find a way to keep his mark, to make it permanent and keep him with me. The logical part wants to rub it away and move on as quickly as he clearly has.

I've never been the sentimental type, the one to swoon and sway over a pretty set of eyes and a nice ass. A perfect, biteable, delicious ass, but that's beside the point. How did such a little slip of a man fall at my feet and shift my carefully controlled world on its axis so quickly and completely that I feel like I don't know who I am anymore now that he's gone? It's been a handful of days, not even, since I first saw him on his knees at my feet on that damn dock. Love at first sight isn't a concept I believe in, something I have ever bought into. Lust at first sight, sure. Infatuation, why not. But full-on love? There's no way.

Love is hard won, and hard-fought, but worth it when you manage to build it. Build it, not have it fall at your feet on a random Friday in January, and then refuse to get in the damn water while on a dive. My parents had it. They loved each other fiercely and fought for that love tooth and nail. It took work and understanding, and there was never a day that went by when I didn't see them be thankful for that love and the work that went into building it.

With a growl, I shove my feet into my shoes and tug my shirt off the chair and over my head before storming out of the room. I have better things to do than sit here and pine over someone who didn't see a point in sparing an extra thought for me.

"What the hell is up your ass, dude?"

It's been two weeks since Gabriel left me in that hotel room, and I have done my best to avoid any inter-action with the guys, preferring to hole up in my room as much as possible. I even volunteered to take a group out on a longer trek earlier this week just to get away from the prying eyes of my friends. Four days with a group of dude-bros from the mainland might not have been my definition of fun, but at least they didn't try to get me to talk about my shitty, confusing feelings.

Clearly my luck has run out though, because when I turn my head to look toward Teo from my spot in the hammock off the back deck, my best friend is staring down at me with a mix of pity and disgust. Just the look you always want to see on someone's face when they look at you.

"I'll ask again, since your ears and your brain have clearly been disconnected lately. What, the fuck, is up, your ass?" he asks again.

"Don't know what you're talking about. I'm fine," I say, trying to deflect.

"Don't give me that shit. If you're not stomping

around like a raging bull with a hot poker up his nuts, then you're moping and sighing like some lovesick little thirteen-year-old girl. Honestly, I don't know which one I hate more. But they both worry me. That's not the Cade I've known since diapers, man."

"Yeah, well, not sure what to tell ya," I grumble, not liking how accurate his description of my attitude is.

"Bullshit. You think you're the only one blindsided by those two?"

That catches my attention. Teo and I haven't talked since Gabriel left, I haven't really talked to anyone, so it's news that he is feeling some kind of way about Deepa leaving too. Maybe it makes me a shit friend, but it never even occurred to me that he might be going through it too. I don't think he and Dee got quite as... familiar... as Gabriel and I did, but they certainly spent plenty of time bickering and poking at one another whenever occupying the same space. Now that I think about it, just about every time I had been with Gabriel, Dee and Teo had been off doing god knows what.

Well, fuck. Now I feel like an even bigger asshole.

My realization must show on my face because Teo lets out a barking laugh. "Yeah, just dawned on ya, huh, jackass?"

"Sorry, man. I've been... it just... he just... my head's been fucked."

"No shit, sherlock. I never wouldda guessed that the love of your damn life flying in and outta your life in the blink of a damn eye would leave you a bit fucked in the head?" he asks, flopping his ass into a lawn chair.

"Gee, don't bother sugar-coating it, Te."

"Nope, got no patience for this shit anymore. I've let you wallow and mope for long enough. At this point,

I'm not sure which of you I'm more pissed at. Him for doin my boy dirty like that, or you for just rolling over and accepting the shitty stunt he pulled most likely while in a panic instead of fighting for what you want. The Cade I know has never backed down from a fight. So why the fuck are you doing it now?"

"Jesus christ Teo, how do you really feel?" Without looking over at him, I can hear him suck in a breath like he is ramping up for another round, but I head him off. "I know, I know. I don't know what's gotten into me, but I can't seem to shake it. He fucked me up, man. I never thought... I never..."

"You never thought love could hit you over the head like a ton of bricks. I know, we all know. You've worked so hard to keep yourself apart, to keep yourself from feeling anything more than a fleeting interest in anyone for as long as I've known you. God knows why, and frankly, I don't care why. All I know is that man broke through to you. He woke something up in you, and I've never seen you more alive. Shit like that doesn't come around every day. Someone who, just by their sheer absence, makes you feel this shitty from missing them is worth fighting for."

"When the hell did you get so wise?"

"I've always been the smart one," he says with a wink before standing from his chair and heading back inside without a backward glance.

As much as I hate to admit it, my dumbass best friend might have a point. I have been wallowing in a mass of self-pity for the better part of two weeks. Sure, the morose cloud has lifted here and there, only to be replaced by a fog of bitter anger bordering on hatred. But now, with Teo's words rattling around in my brain,

I see that the bitterness, anger, and even the catastrophic loneliness and sadness are only skin deep. What's really been eating at me is heartbreak.

Fuck me. I love the asshole. And I need to get him back.

CHAPTER FOURTEEN

GABRIEL

SINCE WHEN ARE cabs the absolute slowest form of conveyance on the goddamn planet? Seriously, I am pretty sure it would be faster to walk at this point, or maybe a horse-drawn carriage. Either way, I am confident literally anything would be better than sitting in the back of this damn car.

Three weeks. Three fucking weeks. I swear on Momma Ru Paul and all that is holy that the last three weeks have been the longest, most miserable of my life. Not a single moment has gone by that I have not regretted leaving the way I did. I should have left a goddamn note. A calling card, hell, a fucking cocktail napkin with my number scrawled on it. Anything would have been better than pulling the absolute chickenshit move I did that morning. I would give anything, and I mean anything... including my collection of original broadway cast recording vinyl, even the Sunday in the Park with George signed by the indomitable Bernadette Peters herself... to talk to Cade again.

In the moment, I knew I had to leave, to get some

distance and sort my head out. Honestly, I still stand by that decision but I wish I would have done it better, in a less dramatic, and let's face it, less of a dickwad way. I don't even know if Cade will ever want to talk to me again after that. I wouldn't blame him if he didn't. Honestly, I'm not sure I would give him the time of day again if he pulled that shit on me.

No matter how I parse it or try to rationalize, it all keeps coming back to one solid truth; those days spent with Cade were the best days of my life. I know, the level of cliche in that sentence is positively gag-worthy, but it's the truth. I'm not one to dwell on, much less talk about my less-than-stellar upbringing, but being the only queer kid in a small, horribly conservative midwestern town was... less than ideal. Being the only son of said town's hyper-conservative staunch evangelical pastor was nothing short of a nightmare. Sparing myself the inevitable heartache and migraine that comes from thinking about that time, let's just go with the story I tell now... I burst into existence at 16 as the fully formed fabulous diva I am today; nothing that happened before matters.

Since bursting onto the scene at 16, it's been one uphill battle after setback after disappointment in just about every arena, but at least I looked great through it all. I am damn proud of everything I've accomplished—I finished high school while living out of the back of a friend's car, put myself through college, and have decently well in my career by just about anyone's standards. But while all of that may be true, and I've been more or less content through it all, I can't say I've ever been truly happy. Looking back, there isn't a single day of my life that I can call a truly happy one... until I met Cade on that damn dock.

That man waltzed in with his board shorts and aviators, his laugh that sucks all the air from a room in the best way and makes my heart race at the same time. His smile reminds me that being happy is a thing that could be within reach for a normal human like myself. From that first moment looking up at him from my knees, when he cocked that damn brow at me, I knew I was lost. For the first time in my life, I felt like there was a light at the end of the endless tunnel that is the day-to-day grind.

"Heya, man, we're here." The lazy voice of the rideshare driver snaps me back to the present, and I look outside, noticing for the first time we are parked on the street outside Cade's house. It's a cloudy, rainy, dreary day, but I have to admit it's hard to remember that it's quickly moving into February. It also feels horribly cliche to be pulling a move like this in this weather, but never let it be said Gabriel Kinghorn doesn't have a flair for the dramatics.

"Can you just... hang on for a second? I need... I need to..." my confidence escapes me completely in the face of actually having to open this car door and face down the next few minutes. For some reason, I can't even muster a full sentence to the rideshare driver who has literally less than zero stake in this situation.

"Sscool, bro. No where I gotta be in this weather. Surf ain't worth it today," the driver says with a laugh that makes me question the gummies I saw him munching when he picked me up. Whatever, I made it here in one piece, so more power to him. God, maybe I should ask him if there are any left. I sure as hell could use some chill right about now.

"Yeah, thanks. I'll be back to grab my stuff just... don't drive off, yeah?" I ask, not entirely trusting he will remember he's supposed to be waiting for me if I leave right now. The whole 'out of sight, out of mind' adage feels very fitting for him at the moment.

"No worries, man. I'll be here," he says, reaching to turn up the classic rock station before reclining his seat back till he's all but lying down. Alrighty then, one high as fuck local sleeping in the driveway was totally not how I thought this would go but, whatever.

Taking a deep breath, I steel myself for whatever is about to happen before pushing open the car door and running up the driveway. Normally I would whine and flail, bitching about the rain ruining my hair or melting my makeup, but right now, I couldn't care less. Everything that's happened in the last three weeks has been leading up to this moment, and I just want to get it over with.

The plan I had so carefully concocted on the long flight over here, the one where I ring the doorbell and have an eloquent speech prepared that I am able to deliver in a dignified manner, goes flying out the damn window when I skid to a halt on the damp concrete of his walkway, the toe of my sneaker catching on the edge of the doormat and I crash face first against the front door.

Wow. Graceful, thy name is Gabe.

Before I can fully recover, much less compose myself enough to knock, the door opens, and I stumble forward into a massive wall of muscle. I take a deep breath before I look up to see which unfortunate soul I literally fell into, hoping against hope it's the one man who might find my ridiculous fumbling even slightly endearing. No luck, the brick wall of a man I'm currently face to t-shirt covered nipple with smells nothing like my memories, and the deep, deep laugh rumbling from him is nothing like the smooth as chocolate voice I'm dying to hear again.

"CADE! You've got a visitor, man!" Siggy bellows over his shoulder into the house as he grabs my shoulders and pushes me away, helping me find my feet again. I struggle not to meet his eyes, the horrified blush I feel burning up my throat and over my cheeks enough to steal any semblance of an apology I might have been able to muster.

If the mortification of my entrance wasn't enough to erase every last thought in my mind and all but liquify my knees, the sight of Cade standing in the archway between the living room and kitchen over Siggy's shoulder, a can of soda frozen halfway to his mouth as he stared slack-jawed back at me definitely does it.

Without a word, the tension between us snaps, and we rush to close the gap, crashing together in the middle of his living room. I vaguely register the sound of his soda can hitting the floor and voices rising in displeasure, but nothing sticks in my mind except him. Our arms wrap around one another, grasping, tugging, clinging to whatever we can reach, hanging on for dear life as our lips collide. Instantly, our tongues tangle together in a desperate, devouring kiss.

I melt when I feel his lips on mine, his tongue taking control of the kiss, and his warmth surrounding me. Everything from the last three weeks comes crashing down, and I lose it. Sobbing into the kiss, I pull him closer, grappling my way up his body as I climb him like a tree. My awkward movements aren't enough to get my legs up around his hips on my own, but he reaches down and grips the backs of my thighs, effortlessly lifting me as the last of my strength fails me, and I am forced to pull away from the kiss. Gasping, I bury my face in his neck as the sobs take over, wracking my body in a shuddering emotional release, the likes of which I don't think I have ever experienced.

Everything is wrapped up in that singular moment; the sorrow of leaving him, the crushing loneliness and isolation I felt the moment I stepped on the plane headed home, and the devastating moment I realized I wasn't flying toward home but away from it. The utter joy and hopeful excitement I felt as I turned in my two weeks' notice the moment I walked into work that first day back. The frustration and anger in dealing with the hooping and bullshit of finishing work and breaking the lease on my shitty apartment. The giddy sense of possibility that came from packing up everything I cared about and getting on that plane this morning to come back to him.

But most of all, the feeling of indescribable relief at the feel of his arms around me, the sense of truly coming home for the first time in my entire life. The feeling of being so utterly, completely, head over heels in love with the man in my arms.

I'm not sure how long I sob against Cade's shoulder, clinging to him like some crazed barnacle, but I slowly return to myself, registering the soothing motion of his hand running along my spine and the whispered words of comfort he is mumbling against my hair. With a final shaky breath, I gather myself enough to look up into the face of the man I am absolutely mad for and hope beyond hope he feels the same.

The hand that had been stroking my back comes to rest against the nape of my neck as Cade stares back at me, pulling me in closer until our foreheads connect, and I hear him utter one simple word. "Why?"

It's the one question I knew to expect and the one I most dread answering, but it's also the one he most deserves answers to. "I needed to sort my shit out. I know I should have done it better, should have talked to you, should have said anything, or even left a goddamned note. Hell, leaving a flip-flop behind like some ratchet gay Cinderfella would have been better than the shit I pulled. As soon as I got home, no, as soon as I set foot on that airplane, I knew. I knew I wasn't heading home. I was heading away from it. Stepping into my apartment felt like entering a stranger's place. Everything felt foreign and wrong. That wasn't where I was supposed to be anymore."

"What does that mean?" Cade asks. The hopeful but restrained note in his voice gives me the confidence to say what needs to come next and trust that maybe, just maybe, he is in this just as deeply as I am.

"It means, my dear sweet, growly Daddy, that my home... where I belong isn't back there. It's wherever your grumpy ass is." I hold my breath. My eyes are still squeezed shut tight as I wait for his response; not sure I could handle it if he rejects me after all this.

"Gonna have to spell it out for me, baby shark," he says, his voice catching on some emotion I am afraid to place, but the slight tightening of his hold on my neck lets me know it's safe to continue.

"It means I'm done chasing sunsets." I lean in and

press a quick kiss to his lips, finally opening my eyes to look at him. "It means that wherever you are," I kiss him again, "that's where I want to be." another kiss. "If you'll have me."

The look of shock melts from his face as he catches me with my next kiss, deepening the contact and kissing me back fiercely.

When we finally have to come up for air, I ask, "Does that mean I can stay?" needing to hear the confirmation from his perfect lips.

Cade throws his head back on a loud, barking laugh for a moment before looking back at me, pressing another kiss to the tip of my nose before answering. "Of course, you fucking can. Want you, need you with me."

"Good, cuz there is a very crabby uber driver waiting outside with a metric ton of my shit in his car waiting for you and your big strong manly men friends here to bring inside," I say with a cheeky smile, all worry and tension officially melting from me at last. I wiggle my way out of his hold and straighten my clothing before turning toward the door, praying the high as fuck driver is still napping at the curb.

Cade pulls me up short by grabbing my hand with a quick tug, turning me back to face him. "Wait, does this make me the Patrick to your David, then?"

Sweet RuPaul, mother of all things good and holy.

"Did... did you just make a Schitt's Creek reference?" I ask, astounded.

"Tell me I'm wrong! Also, don't look so shocked. I dare you to show me a single millennial that hasn't binge-watched Schitt's Creek at least a dozen times," he says with a laugh before tugging me in close once again for another kiss.

A sharp gasp and cry of "Ewww David!" in a ridiculous put-on voice from somewhere behind us has us pulling away in a fit of laughter.

"Well played, guys, well played," I say, looking over Cade's shoulder and acknowledging the guys sitting around the living room watching some football game or something.

"Come on, let's go get your crap," Cade says, tugging me toward the door. He leans down and growls against my ear as we step out onto the walkway. "Fuck baby, I'm gonna redden that ass of yours so good for leaving like that."

"Promises, promises, Daddy."

Six Months Later

CADE.

The moment my head breaks the surface, I pull out my respirator and throw my head back, laughing up at the evening sky, only now starting to catch fire with subtle hues of pink and red. I lean back, letting the BC take over the work of floating as I laugh, waiting for Gabriel to surface. Less than a minute later, his head, crowned in a mass of liquid silver curls, pops up a couple of arm lengths away. His respirator is ripped from his mouth, and goggles are shoved up in seconds before he lets out an ear-splitting squeal. His eyes are shining brighter than I think I have ever seen them and the smile gracing his perfect face is dazzling as he paddles his way toward me. When he's within reach, he grabs the straps of my BC and tugs me closer before all but screaming in my face.

"Did you see it?! You saw it, right? It was right there! It was so beautiful! And so HUGE! I think I could have ridden the damn thing like a pony!" Even through all the gear and gentle buffeting of the waves, I can feel him all but vibrate from excitement.

"Yeah, baby, I saw it. Are you forgetting I'm the one who had to all but rip your regulator out to get your attention and point it out to you?" I can't help but chuckle at his indignant squeak as he pushes me away slightly and slaps water in my face.

"You did not! I was distracted by the ray below me at that specific moment. Doesn't mean I would have missed the BIGGEST DAMN TURTLE IN EXIS-TENCE for much longer," he huffs in defense. To be fair, he might be right, but I still find it incredibly enter-taining that we have been diving at least twice a week for the entire six months since he moved here, and this was the first time he had a chance to see a turtle, and he almost missed it.

Gabe has been absolutely obsessed with seeing a turtle since that first dive we took while he was on his trip. I honestly can't say what he is so hyped up about when it comes to them, other than that he might be the only person on the island who hadn't seen one until now. But today, while we were down there, I saw a beautiful old dude of a turtle coming over a rise in the coral and knew Gabriel would have my balls if I let him miss it. I tried waving to get his attention and got up in front of him to try again when it didn't work the first time. When it still didn't work, I pulled up alongside him and tapped his shoulder, hoping the contact would snap him out of whatever he was fixating on, but that only earned me a distracted slap-ping in my general direction without him even looking my way. He *finally* deigned to look at me after I grabbed his wrist and tugged hard. I am not one to condone roughhousing while diving, but for the sake of not letting my boyfriend miss his damn turtle and having to sleep on the couch, I made an exception. When Gabriel finally looked over at the turtle, I swear I could hear his squeal of delight even while 60 feet below the surface.

"You don't understand, though, babe! Did you see how gorgeous he was? I swear one of his flippers was the size of my damn head!" Gabriel's excitement is damn infectious, and I can't help but smile, laughing again.

"You know, it's rather presumptuous of you to assume the turtle's gender." I can't help teasing him. It's really just too easy sometimes, and when he's all riled up like this is my favorite.

Gabe's horrified gasp as he clutches at imaginary pearls has me cackling. "Oh my Gaga! You're... wait. You're fucking with me. Asshole," he grumbles, reaching for me and pressing on my shoulders, briefly dunking me back below the surface.

Spluttering a laugh as I pop back up, I take a quick mouthful of water and shoot it back at him in a jet, getting him right in the face. "Oh, you are so gonna pay for that, Daddy!" he screeches, wiping the saltwater from his eyes with a scowl, though the intimidating effect is completely ruined by the teasing light in his eyes and a bright smile still breaking across his face.

Before he can retaliate, I am swimming away, high-tailing it back to the boat. I am up on the dive platform and almost have my BC unbuckled by the time he catches up, any heat gone from his laugh. We make quick work of stripping out of and stowing our dive equipment and settle onto the bow, a picnic spread out around us once again.

This has become one of our favorite pastimes, spending a lazy evening on the boat together, sharing a picnic, and watching the sun set over the waves. I have lost count of the times we have come out to do exactly this in the last six months, and I can honestly say they have become some of the best moments of my life. From the moment he stumbled back into my life, it's been nonstop with Gabriel. Between getting him settled, of course, in my house because fuck if I was going to let him out of my sight again, and him working with the guys and me to get the business up and going, these evening sails have been some of the few moments of peace we manage to steal together.

Looking back, I never would have dreamed I would end up where I am right now, with a thriving business that I own with my best friends and the absolute love of my life, living the life I always wanted but never believed was actually within my reach. Not a day goes by that I am not grateful for the little ball of chaotic energy currently curled up against my chest.

I lean down and brush a kiss against his temple in a moment of pure sentimentality. "I love you, baby shark."

"Love you too, Daddy."

The End

ACKNOWLEDGMENTS

First off, Jackie, my twin, my soul sister. Nothing about this book would have been possible without you. Not a single word would have gotten written if it weren't for your love, support, and borderline abusive (in the best way) brand of encouragement.

Kayla and Randee, you two round out our little group and the unwavering support and never-ending stream of weird gifs and memes give me life.

All my love to my amazing betas: Jackie, Kayla, Randee, Gretchen, and Jes. I adore you all and watching you guys fall in love with these boys as much as I have makes everything worth it.

To K, my amazing cover designer, thank you for putting up with my last minute late night insanity when it came to this cover. You absolutely knocked it out of the park and I am obsessed with everything you do.

Last but certainly not least, to my wonderful hubster. Thank you for putting up with my scatter-brained ridiculousness when I get lost in a story, your support and understanding when it comes to giving me the space and ability to explore my passion, and for not citing the mountain of unwashed dishes in any future letters of complaint or divorce filings ☺ (Oh I'm only joking.. you're stuck with me forever mwhahahah)

J.E. Joyce lives in the frozen hellscape *cough* sorry, the lovely snow-covered dreamscape that is Minnesota. She is an unrepentant coffee addict, lifelong Broadway fanatic and theater geek, and thinks Deadpool absolutely counts as a chick flick. When she isn't melting pages with the steamy dreamy book boyfriends in her head, she's annoying the ever-loving heck outta her hubster and two mini monsters.